Death Rides the Denver Stage

A Western Story

G·K
Hall
&Co.

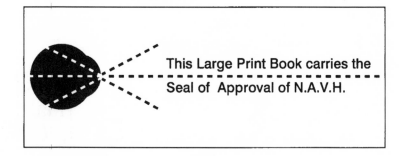

Death Rides the Denver Stage

A Western Story

LEWIS B. PATTEN

G.K. Hall & Co. • Thorndike, Maine

Published in 2000 by arrangement with
Golden West Literary Agency.

G.K. Hall Large Print Western Series.

The text of this Large Print edition is unabridged.
Other aspects of the book may vary from the original edition.

Set in 16 pt. Plantin by Minnie B. Raven.

Printed in the United States on permanent paper.

Library of Congress Cataloging-in-Publication Data

Patten, Lewis B.
    Death rides the Denver Stage : a western story / Lewis B. Patten.
      p. cm.
    ISBN 0-7838-8399-4 (lg. print : hc : alk. paper)
    1. Colorado — Fiction. 2. Large type books. I. Title.
  PS3566.A79 D428   2000
  813′.54—dc21   00-027586

Death Rides the Denver Stage

A Western Story

Chapter One

The shades of dusk lent a softness to this harsh, new land, brought welcome coolness after the long day of the blazing sun's heat. It turned the distant mountains deep blue-gray and brought a stiff breeze from the west, a breeze that took dust from beneath the coach's yellow wheels and whisked it away to one side. It was at dusk that red-bearded Cass Leary wheeled the stage into a way station for a last change of horses. Of the distance to Denver City, there now remained only the tag end, a short twenty miles which would be covered in evening's early darkness.

The passengers filed from the coach, staggered with weariness, fully exhausted as only human flesh can become after a week of rattling about the interior of a lurching, jolting Concord. Ten feet from the coach the girl stumbled, and Cletus Fahr, immediately behind her, reached out a steadying hand. Her murmured — "Thank you." — was almost lost in the harsh shouting of the hostler as he led the teams away. Yet the tone of her voice was soft, rich, holding its overtones of irrepressible humor.

Clee smiled. He liked her matter-of-fact, uncomplaining manner. It was as though she faced all of life, both good and bad, with warm and smiling approval. Steadying her elbow, he

7

walked along with her toward the low door of the adobe way station. It was a squat and unlovely building, behind which were pole corrals for the horses, an adobe shed for hay, and behind that a draw where a thin trickle of water made its faint shine in the fading light.

Inside the building a couple of lamps glowed. Beside the door, held in place by nails driven into the adobe bricks, was a handbill. Clee handed the girl into the doorway, then with mild and idle boredom brought his face close to the handbill and read:

Arms wanted.
Highest prices paid.
Eames Jeffords.
Fremont House, Denver City.

Not an easy name, Eames Jeffords. Not a name you encountered everyday. Clee scowled, remembering hatred and bitterness, recalling violence and death.

Behind him the big man, Herman Spicer, moved up, deliberately jostling him, although he had read the notice over Clee's shoulder — Spicer, who had fished in vain all the way from Bent's Fort for a firm declaration of allegiance from Clee. He pretended to read the notice again, afterward putting his insolent glance on Clee, saying: "A friend of yours, I suppose? A damned Secesh like yourself. Keep your slaves and sedition in the South where they belong, my

8

friend. We're free men in Colorado, and we'll remain that way." He stood in the doorway, back to the light, a big and solid man, black-bearded and challenging, plainly hoping for a fight.

Another time, Clee might have laughed off his challenge. Tonight, he felt a strange wildness caused by the memories Jeffords's name had invoked, felt it rising in intemperate anger. He said softly: "Why damn you, man, I guess there's only one language you understand."

Spicer growled: "You're Union, or you're Secesh, and there ain't no in between. Not in my book, there ain't."

Clee, grinning now, said — "I'll make one then." — and came forward with an easy bound, rising as the ground rose to the doorway. His left went out, sank into Spicer's belly, then the point of his shoulder drove against the big man's chest, forcing him back into the softly lighted room.

Action, after twenty-four hours of pounding his buttocks against a hard coach seat, was a welcome thing. Even the smash of Spicer's big fist against his head he found welcome and oddly pleasant. His right went out, found a solid mark, and Spicer went back again, this time falling into the heavy curtain that separated the room into two parts. His heel caught in it. His body fell against it, and the whole thing came down, showing Clee a brief glimpse of the girl's white petticoat, of her trim ankles beneath its ruffled hem. She gave a light, short cry, and then snatched up her heavy dress and held it before her.

Clee's grin widened, watching her, his lively interest caught and held by her startled beauty. She was a small girl, although full of breast and round of hip. High cheekbones gave her cheeks the faintest hollow cast, collecting soft shadows. Her eyes were now wide and large, being a deep and startling shade of blue. Her lips were full, parting lightly from surprise. *Lips meant for a man's kissing,* thought Clee.

At this exact instant, Spicer, who had fought himself free of the heavy curtain folds, came forward with a head-down rush, fists swinging wildly. His right caught Clee, off guard and still smiling, on the side of his head. Clee's neck cracked from the force of the blow. His mouth filled with a brassy, unpleasant taste. As though flung sideways by some monstrous force, he whirled across the room, and was prevented from falling only by the rough solidness of the adobe wall.

A high, thin voice cried from the door: "Hey! Hey! Can't you do that outside?"

After this, Clee heard Cass Leary's deep chuckle, his deep, booming voice: "No need for that. It'll be over in a minute. A man can't fight and look at a woman at the same time."

Spicer came at Clee again. Clee shook his head to clear the stunned stupidity from it. His face was flaming. He felt foolish, caught like this, gawking at a girl, although he had to admit it had been worth it. It wasn't every day you saw a girl like that with her dress off. Still, there was this business at hand, this Spicer. Spicer, with more enthusiasm than skill, came rushing in, roaring his sheer delight. There was a dangerous glow in his narrowed eyes.

Clee stepped away from the wall to meet him, a tall man in his late twenties whose clothes concealed a long-muscled toughness, yet who appeared too light to stand and slug it out with the weight and power that Spicer possessed. He slowed the Northerner with a stiff left to the belly, then straightened him with an upswinging right. He took Spicer's battering, poorly aimed blows on shoulders and arms, meanwhile jolting stiff rights and lefts to the man's unprotected face.

Blood spurted redly from Spicer's nose, crimsoned his beard beneath it, and dripped down onto his shirt. An animal growl of hurt and rage rumbled in his chest at this, and a hand went roughly across his mouth to clear the blood away.

Cletus caught a glimpse, from the corner of his eye, of the girl, scrambling into her dress, and thinking — "This is too good to miss." — put all of his attention and all of his strength into his next two blows, blows which put Spicer down on the dirt floor, stunned but not out. Clee Fahr then leaned back against the wall, laughing softly and drawing deep, gusty breaths of air into his lungs. His buckskin shirt was torn, exposing a powerfully rounded shoulder, very white in contrast to his darkly tanned face.

11

The girl, Nanette Massey, arms through the skirt of her dress, threw him a beseeching glance that was touched with anger, then dropped the dress over her head. Still it was not buttoned, and Clee caught a glimpse of the crescents of her upper breasts, an enticing glimpse that raised a faint, pink color to his face. She turned her back in exasperation, and Clee laughed aloud. As always, there was a loose relaxation about him, coupled with deep, personal interest in all that went on.

Spicer was struggling to his knees, and now Clee watched him, gauging the amount of temper which might be left. This fight was pointless, and not of his choosing. He knew he could fight Spicer until the stage's departure time, and so miss his supper, or he could find a way to stop it now. The first choice had little appeal for him, since he did not particularly dislike Spicer. Besides, he was hungry. The scrawny station-keeper's clumsy efforts to replace the curtain gave him the opening he sought. As Spicer rose to his feet, glaring, Clee walked past him, muttering: "We knocked the damned thing down. Least we can do is to put it back."

Spicer grumbled sourly: "Bucko, we ain't quite finished."

But Clee ignored him and came up beside the station-keeper. He said: "I'm taller. Let me pull it up."

The curtain had been hung from a rope stretched at ceiling height across the room. Replacing it was simply a matter of passing it over the rope and drawing the upper end down until its weight would hold it in place.

While Spicer scowled, and Clee grinned, they heard the brief splash of water behind the curtain, and shortly afterward Nanette Massey, fully dressed, moved out into the main part of the room. She averted her eyes from Clee. Her face held the faint shine of its recent washing, and the hair at her forehead, wholly black, was slightly damp. A Mexican woman waddled into the room, bearing a huge and steaming crock of chili, then returned to the lean-to kitchen at the rear of the station for coffee.

The station-keeper spoke sourly, saying: "Wash water's out back fer the men."

Cass Leary, shoulder point against the door jamb, growled good-naturedly: "Make it quick. Ten minutes is all that's left."

Clee went around the corner of the building with Spicer immediately behind him. It was easy enough, these days, to get into a political argument. Yet argument never changed opinion. Anger, as he thought of the way he had been forced into this argument, rose in Clee. He splashed water into his face, scrubbed briskly, then spoke to the sullen Spicer: "Don't force a man to argue with you, my friend." He waited, while Spicer finished scrubbing the blood from his beard. Then he said: "I was raised in the North. I've got friends in the South. Up to now, I haven't taken either side. But I will. By God I will

13

take sides, if anybody tries to crowd me."

Spicer stared at him, but did not seem inclined to pursue the matter further. Clee turned on his heel and went back around the station. He was puzzling about Jeffords. Knowing the man, he was aware that there could be but one reason for his thus openly purchasing guns. Jeffords was a Southern aristocrat, his loyalty unquestionable. So even here the conflict raged, if not yet openly. Clee might have guessed as much.

Behind him, Spicer called — "Wait." — and Clee halted warily.

Spicer came up, a hulking shape in near darkness. He stuck out a huge paw, saying: "All right. Maybe you ain't solid North. But at least you ain't Secesh. Can a man say he might have been hasty?"

Clee took the hand. "Sure. Forget it." The atmosphere was strained, and more from the need to ease it than anything else Clee asked: "You a Denver man?"

"Why, I guess you might say I was. I been here three years. Took a turn at the mines. When that didn't work, I started a store. Hardware. I been East on a buyin' trip."

"Mostly Northern folks in Denver?"

Spicer nodded. "Mostly. There's plenty of damned Rebels to stir up trouble, though. Like that Jeffords."

"What's he buying guns for?"

Spicer's beard glistened with water in the fading light. His face, all but hidden behind it,

14

was grim. "He's arming the Secesh element. By God, I don't know why it is, but Union men in this country will sell their guns. The Rebels won't. You see what that's doin', don't you?" He gave Clee no time to answer, instead answered his own question. "It arms the Rebels, disarms the Union men. The governor, Gilpin, might just as well be helpin' them, because he's buyin' guns, too. 'Fore long, between Jeffords and the governor, they'll have all the Union guns and then the damned Rebels'll take over."

Clee murmured: "We better go eat, if we're going to."

He moved around the corner to the front door. Nanette Massey sat at one end of the table, and Clee took the place beside her, eyes glinting mischievously. The Mexican woman stolidly ladled chili onto his plate and poured his tin cup full of coffee.

Ravenous, Clee ate. Yet Eames Jeffords lingered disturbingly at the back of his mind, bringing a flood of unwelcome memories, turning his face bitter and brooding. As though it had all been yesterday, he could recall the tall, lean figure of Jeffords, the ink-black hair, the olive skin, and patrician features. Nor could he ever remember Jeffords without also remembering Sibyl McAllister, lovely, fragile, and the background, the setting in which he had known them both — high-columned plantation manors, hot, broad fields of cotton, dark, cool forests of pine.

Recalling Jeffords could bring to Cletus the

15

memory of a savage, killing rage, of a duel where a split second of treachery on Jeffords's part had meant the difference between victory and vengeance and months in the hospital for Clee. Now he was to see Jeffords again. It was all to come back — those things so assiduously forgotten. For the briefest moment, he wondered about Sibyl, and then all of it was alive again in Clee, the fire, the passion, the longing. The fragrance of flowers, the shouted laughter of the blacks in the fields, the cool evenings. . . . He shook his head savagely.

Cass Leary rose from the table. "All right. Next stop, Denver City."

Clee caught the puzzled glance of Herman Spicer, studying him. The man was not yet satisfied. Nanette Massey went out of the door into night's soft darkness, moving with the easy grace which was so characteristic of her. The miner, Fannin, followed her, and Clee walked behind him and beside Spicer.

Fannin had made a fortune in the mines, had taken it East, and had it taken away from him neatly. Undismayed, he was back, fully confident that he could take a second fortune from the gravelly bed of the Vasquez as easily as he had taken the first.

Spicer, carefully prying, asked as Clee helped Nanette into the coach: "Been trappin'? Or prospectin'? You been at Bent's Fort long?"

"Not long," answered Clee cryptically, and climbed into the coach.

Spicer followed, taking the seat beside Nanette. Fannin sat across from her, Clee beside Fannin. Cass Leary lighted the side-lamps and climbed up to the box. With a heavy lurch, the coach rumbled into motion, swiftly picked up speed until the horses were at a steady gallop. His whip popped sharply, and the monotony of the man's steady cursing began.

Spicer watched Clee steadily.

Nanette Massey murmured: "You will save us all trouble, if you'll give him a short history of your life."

Spicer flushed unhappily. He grumbled something unintelligibly, and in spite of his irritation Clee made a tight smile. He said: "He doesn't care about my life. But he's almighty curious about what I've been doing in Texas." He stared at Spicer. "I'll tell you. My father had seven brothers. They all had sons. That gave me quite a few cousins. One of them happens to live in Texas. He runs cattle. I've been down there visiting. There was a matter of cattle stealing that was bothering him. I helped him out with it."

"And he sent you up here to spy for the Rebels."

Clee shook his head patiently. Nanette Massey was smiling openly, and he grinned back. Spicer was obviously beginning to feel ridiculous. Clee said: "I didn't like Texas. I don't care for cattle. So I left. I am unemployed at the moment." He stared blandly at Spicer until the man dropped his glance.

Clee settled back against the seat corner and pulled his broad-brimmed hat over his eyes. There would be no sleep for him tonight, yet at least the appearance of sleep would gain him the privacy of his own thoughts. What the hell was Eames Jeffords doing in Denver City? What was behind this business of buying guns?

A slight suspicion, soon discarded, formed in Clee's mind. No, in spite of the treachery of the dueling ground, Jeffords was no coward. Unscrupulous, perhaps, but not cowardly. Therefore, his place should have been with the Georgia cavalry, with his neighbors and friends, fighting for their homeland. And another question posed itself. Was Sibyl with Jeffords?

At this thought excitement stirred Cletus unwillingly until he beat it down. Spicer said patiently, stolidly: "A man has got to declare himself, and a little tussle clears up nothing at all."

Clee snatched his hat from his face and sat up straight. For a moment utter wildness flared in his eyes. He said harshly: "Let it go, you damned fool! Let it go. I told you I was born in the North."

"But you said you had relatives in the South. How many, my friend, and what would you do for them?"

Nanette Massey's voice, unconcerned, broke the dark silence. "Mister Spicer! Let it go for tonight. It is too crowded for fighting here, and, if you don't be quiet, there will surely be fighting."

Fannin piped sleepily: "No more of that now. No more of that!"

Spicer subsided, growling sourly. Clee, flushed with his sudden, volatile anger, grinned wryly, unwillingly, and thought: *Lord! The man's a damned mastiff. He'll hang onto this and worry it until he's firmly convinced I'm nothing but a damned spy.*

He felt sure he could clear up Spicer's doubt by a simple and hearty declaration of allegiance. Stubbornness would prevent that, and, even if it did not, uncertainty would. Clee frankly did not know where he stood in regard to the conflict. A man owed something to his homeland, to the land of his birth. He owed something as well to his friends and relations, whose hospitality he had accepted a hundred times.

Spicer kept up his grumbling, but carefully did not direct his statements at Clee. "A bunch of damned, seditious traitors," he muttered. "Buying guns in Colorado, minin' gold on the Vasquez, and then smugglin' it into the South. Even the damned fool governor of the territory is playin' into their hands. I tell you we've got enough of them in our midst, spyin', sneakin' around. . . ."

Fannin said: "Shut up. Let a man sleep."

Spicer subsided again impotently, but Clee could see in the angry set of his expression, the working of his agitated and suspicious mind.

The miles rolled past, monotonously, regularly. The coach lurched and tossed, bounded

19

into the air and descended with bone-jarring crashes. Nanette Massey, sleeping finally, rolled against Spicer, and the man gently shoved her away. A full moon, dark yellow, poked above the eastern horizon, bathing the stark and empty plain with its golden glow. Yet Spicer's scowl remained, and the tortured memories in Cletus would not fade.

The Concord rolled into Denver City and drew up at ten-thirty before the Fremont House amid a cloud of dust, a thunderous clatter of plunging hoofs, and the profane shouts of Cass Leary. Nanette Massey awoke at this, sitting up, her wide eyes filled with startled confusion and sudden fright.

Clee said softly — "Denver City." — opened the door, and stepped down. Spicer sprang out, ponderously agile, and then the girl alighted on Clee's arm. Hostlers came from the hotel and began to unload baggage from the boot. Behind the girl, his face as still and calm as stone, Clee walked into the lighted lobby.

Chapter Two

There are times when, seeing a well-known face, all things associated with it become sharp and clear to a man, and time stands still, while his racing mind relives the past. Thus it was with Cletus Fahr as he stepped into the ornate lobby of the Fremont House. Directly across the carpeted lobby was the desk with its pigeonholes for mail and its rack for keys behind it. To the right was the hotel dining room, empty and dark at this hour, to the left was the bar.

Nanette Massey, without pausing, with weariness putting a slight sag to her straight shoulders, swept across the floor toward the desk. Herman Spicer came past Clee with an unsatisfied scowl. Fannin had slunk off downstreet in search of less expensive accommodations.

Clee paused in the doorway, let his glance rove over the crowd in the lobby, let it sweep through the wide archway to the bar. He made a noticeable figure there, indolent, seemingly relaxed, yet fully self-possessed. He was all long, loose, relaxed muscles, yet the tension was plain in him, too — tension of the mind perhaps, tension of spirit. His garb was a mixture of a mountain man's fringed and beaded buckskins, darkened with travel dust and sweat, of Texas cowman's boots, of broad-brimmed cavalry hat. About his middle he wore a leather belt and a holstered Colt percussion revolver. From this belt dangled a powder flask and a buckskin shot punch. On his left side he wore a short-bladed, bone-handled knife.

He would have known that slim, stiff-backed figure at the bar even if he had not been halfway expecting it. So he moved that way, feeling savage and strange, with all of the things that had happened so many years before racing headlong before his mind.

Eames Jeffords, after all of these years, was unchanged. And sight of Jeffords, so poignantly associated with Sibyl in Clee's mind, brought her before him as well, beautiful, so beautiful, brought, too, the unwelcome picture of a cousin's sightless eyes staring upward into an early morning sky. Sight of Jeffords brought back a youth's feel for beautiful things that are gone, gaiety, dances and parties, headlong rides, drinking, and banqueting. It was like living it all over again, yet as Clee reached the wide arch and paused, only one part of the vision remained, that of Jeffords, a long, smoking dueling pistol in his hand, looking down at Clee's impetuous, foolishly gallant cousin, Darrel Fahr.

As they had so long ago, again the smoky fumes of rage rose to Clee's brain, turned him wild and reckless. Yet still he stood, motionless, white-faced, while the rest of it returned. All the stupid, useless rest of it. Both Clee and Darrel had been madly in love with Sibyl, or had thought they were, which had led Clee to hold back in favor of his younger cousin, whose guest he was, and Darrel had become engaged to Sibyl. Then had come Jeffords, with his easy certainty of women, holding nothing sacred, smooth-talking Sibyl until she did not even know her own mind. There was a dark balcony, Jeffords with Sibyl in his arms. No more than that. They had been discovered by Darrel, immediately, insanely jealous. A shrill and boyish challenge. Clee's face twisted.

This was the way you did these things, according to a stupid, threadbare code of chivalry that clashed so harshly with the streak of brutal directness in Clee. Clee would have beaten Jeffords insensible with his fists. But it was not Clee's quarrel. It was Darrel who faced Jeffords in the smoky chill of dawn. And what chance had Darrel, just turned nineteen, against this Jeffords, who had a dozen duels behind him?

With Darrel limp as clay on the dewy grass, Clee had sprung at Jeffords, with murder the gentlest of all the emotions in him. Yet before Clee would kill Jeffords with his hands, having no other weapon, they had been pulled apart.

Perhaps tonight, the brutal intensity of Clee's glance warned the man, for Jeffords turned, his smile freezing on his face. When he saw Clee, his hand started its automatic way beneath his gray broadcloth coat.

The subsequent duel between Clee and Jeffords had been something like this, man against man, gun against gun. The code said you started pacing from a back-to-back position. Ten paces each, the steps taken at the count. Then you turned — fired. Clee's murderous rage had by then cooled and turned to ice. He would have put his ball squarely between Jeffords's eyes. But even then there had been a harnessed savagery about Clee that Jeffords had seen and feared. So Jeffords had turned a fraction of a second too soon, had fired as Clee came about.

Clee saw Jeffords's hand halt now, and he said levelly: "Go ahead, Eames. This time it will be different. You know that, don't you?"

The hand under Jeffords's coat flattened and came slowly out — empty. The gesture cheated Clee, turned hate and anger to blind fury. His voice was incredulous. "No! No, God damn your soul! It's not going to be that way!"

Jeffords's forehead took on a faint perspiration shine. He said: "Clee, that's over. That was a long time ago."

Where a moment before the bar had been filled with the busy hum of voices, now it became deathly quiet. Clee's voice shook with controlled fury. "You yellow bastard!" He stared coldly at Jeffords's paling, olive complexion, at the face now distinguished by a flowing, black, cavalry mustache, at the high, patrician forehead, at the hollow cheeks, at the lips that were too red and full for a man's. He said, still deliberately baiting: "You damned renegade! Are the risks as great buying guns as they are dueling with boys?"

At his first epithet, Jeffords's face had paled. Now it colored with instant rage. Clee waited, hoping, and he thought, with no surprise: *Pride! Pride is all he's got. It's part of their damned silly system.*

At first, Clee had blamed Sibyl McAllister as harshly as he blamed Eames Jeffords. Yet passions and judgments cool. Jeffords, utterly unscrupulous where women were concerned, took what he wanted from them, and Sibyl, perhaps entirely innocent of provoking him, might have shrunk from crying out for fear of provoking the very thing which had been the result of their discovery. Afterward, because of the scandal, Sibyl had been sent to Louisiana to visit relatives, and Clee, having spent three long months in the hospital, returned to his home in the North and did not see her again.

With a sense of rising frustration he watched pride fight a losing battle in Jeffords. Here, two thousand miles from Georgia, Jeffords took Clee's harsh estimate of him and made no overt move. Yet, helpless rage was plain in Jeffords, rage that turned his knuckles white and his glare to ice.

Clee knew the man, or thought he did. There was carefulness in Jeffords, but no cowardice. There was the will to survive, and unscrupulousness enough to insure survival, yet, under the goad of such rage as he felt tonight, carefulness should have surrendered to recklessness.

Then why didn't it? What was the thing that held Jeffords in check? Jeffords was working for the interests of the Confederacy, as the handbill proved. And suddenly Clee was doubly sure that there was more to Jeffords's activities than buying guns. Any fool could buy guns, and Jeffords was no fool.

Tonight, Eames had counted his life more valuable than his pride. Then, perhaps, his life was more valuable to the Confederacy than pride was to himself. Clee suddenly recalled a bit of drunken boasting he had heard at a bar in Paradero. Perhaps that was it. Perhaps there had been more truth to that boast than he had at first imagined.

Clee's rage had built him up to a fighting pitch. He said, reluctant to acknowledge his disappointment: "Another time, Eames? When you have an advantage? Or will you shoot me in the back?"

Jeffords's hands were trembling with fury. He placed them against the bar behind him. But he would not speak. Clee shrugged, turned, and walking stiffly as though in a dream, crossed the lobby to the desk.

The slave-holding South was an anachronism, a ridiculous, gallant, incredible anachronism. Nowhere else on earth could this thing have happened, one man dead, another gravely wounded, a woman's life in ruins, all because of a kiss on a moonlit balcony. And the thing was yet unfinished. Before it could be finished, another man must die.

Yet in this summer of 1861, death had become commonplace, and the death of one, or a dozen might well go virtually unnoticed and unheeded.

Chapter Three

Nanette Massey signed the register with her tiny, flowing signature. In spite of the weariness that lay so heavily over every part of her being, her face retained its lively, half-smiling animation, as though nothing, no exhaustion, no physical thing could ever entirely turn it sober. Another woman, perhaps, would have been outraged over Clee's smiling insolence at the way station earlier tonight. Nanette had simply been amused. Only girl in a large family of boys, she had early learned to accept men for what they were, rowdy, exuberant, childish, sometimes dangerous. Too, she had felt instant interest in tall Cletus Fahr when he had boarded the stage at Bent's Fort. She had watched him surreptitiously along the route, divining his wildness and masculine hardness, yet sensing, also, that beneath this was a gentleness that another man would never see.

Thinking of him, she turned and watched his slow advance toward the open doors of the bar. Puzzlement touched her at once, for he had none of the relaxation which a man would normally feel as he approached a bar and a coming drink of fiery liquor. She saw him pause in the doorway, tense and oddly silent. She saw the well-dressed man at the bar turn, saw the paling of his olive-skinned face.

A cold finger of fear touched Nanette, for she had seen her share of violence, and this sight was no stranger to her. Instinct told her at once that these two knew each other, told her as well that they were deadly enemies. A half scream froze in her throat as the dark one's hand went under his coat. Yet Cletus made no move, and his very posture seemed to welcome the impending gun play.

Clee's words, spoken slowly and viciously, were indistinguishable to Nanette, but there was no mistaking their deliberately insulting intent, or the effect they had upon the stranger. His narrow features showed utter, murderous rage for an instant, and then the change came over him, unmistakable, slow, unwilling. At the last Nanette breathed a long, slow sigh of relief.

Clee Fahr came walking toward her as though in a daze, not seeing her, not seeing anything. His eyes were the color of smoke, rising in early sunlight from a wood fire, smoke with a glacial coldness about it, an utter, brutal ruthlessness.

Nanette felt maddened and somehow terribly disappointed. She had seen the humor in Clee; she had sensed his wildness. She had seen his easy gentleness. This vicious hatred she was seeing now disturbed her. He came up beside her and drew the register toward him, signing it quickly and with a flourish. She noticed that his hands were shaking with suppressed fury. He seemed to recognize her presence all at once, and a measure of calm returned to his face, enforced calm as though only his powerful will had put it there. He turned toward her.

She said softly: "You hate him, don't you?"

His eyebrows raised, and his glance was instantly cold.

Anger touched Nanette. She said spiritedly: "Perhaps that was impertinent. But was it any more so that your conduct at the way station tonight?"

She had caught his interest. The smoke color of his eyes lost its glacial cast. His humor was slow in coming. Then his long mouth quirked, and a smile spread across his face. Nanette could feel herself coloring at the warm, personal interest his eyes held for her.

He said wryly: "I'm a product of the North, but I'm damned if I don't act like a Southern fool sometimes." He nodded. "Yes, I hate him all right." He seemed about to go on, but stopped himself with a shrug. "It goes back a long way."

The clerk, unnoticed through this, now spoke to the girl. "Miss Massey, your room is One Twelve. Would you like to go up now?"

She nodded. As she followed the clerk up the great, wide staircase, she asked: "Do you know Sam Massey? He was to have met me. I'm his sister."

The clerk nodded. "Everyone knows Sam Massey. I'll send him word that you're here."

Nanette smiled at this. At the landing she cast one last glance downward at the man in buckskins. He was thumbing the register, several pages back, an intent scowl on his dark-tanned face.

A thousand questions churned in the girl's thoughts. *Who is this Cletus Fahr? What is he doing here? Is he Rebel or Yankee? By his own statement he is of Northern origin. Yet he came up from a cousin's ranch in Texas, admitted to a large number of relatives and friends in the South. Spy? Renegade?* Nanette shook her head. Spicer had entertained doubts about Fahr. Yet in some way Nanette was instantly sure that whatever Clee Fahr did would be done because of a deep conviction that it was right. He was no self-seeker, no opportunist. He might espouse a wrong or lost cause out of loyalty, never from motives baser than that. Nanette was equally sure, however, that once Clee did choose a side in this conflict there would be no holding back, no quibbling over method or means.

Honestly Nanette asked herself: *Which side of the conflict is right?* She admitted the right and wrong on both sides. Slavery was the deep wrong on the part of the South, yet slavery was not an institution born of the South. It went further back than that — to England, to New England, where white men had been held in bondage until it was found that an industrial system worked better without slaves than with them. So far as the North was concerned, then, it was not so much a matter of principle as convenience. Surely, had the North found the slave system as necessary and profitable as the South did, they

31

would have continued it until advancing civilization outmoded it once and for all in the entire country at the same time. Because of this irreconcilable difference in the two systems, now throughout the great country the argument and the conflict continued. Men who had never owned a slave were as vociferous in defense of the system as were those who lived by it. Contrarily, men of the North, slaves to an industrial system in all but name, fought as savagely to stamp out the South's evil as the South fought to preserve it.

Nanette Massey was no meek woman who accepted the edicts and opinions of men as Gospel. She thought things out for herself. She had listened to, and entered into, the endless arguments at home, arguments which had no ultimate solution. She could realize that there was more to the war than the slave question. For the South it was also to be a final decision on states' rights, a fight against a central government that, neither comprehending nor trying to understand a distant state's problems, nevertheless sought to regulate and control them. As the controversy raged, it became more bitter, and the minds of the men were inflamed until they would neither see nor admit the right and justice that existed on both sides.

Nanette shrugged wearily and entered her room, knowing that she herself should bitterly hate the South and all it stood for. At Bull Run, three of her brothers had fallen, and one had been captured. She was fully aware that wars are not fought well by those with analytical and detached minds, that the best soldiers were those who blindly hated and detested the common enemy.

Perhaps her trouble, this ability to see right wherever it existed, was also Clee Fahr's trouble. He had been raised in the North, but had spent a good part of his life, apparently, in the South. He would be torn between the two, hating the thought of fighting friends and perhaps relations on either side. Perhaps he had fled from the bitter decision. No. Nanette shook her head. He did not seem the type of man who would flee from anything.

Abruptly, then, Nanette was surprised and faintly shocked at her own deep interest in this stranger. Her thoughts, since leaving Bent's Fort, she now realized had concerned themselves with little but Cletus Fahr. Tonight, she had hardly considered the joy of seeing her brother Sam again for thinking of Clee.

"He should have met the stage," was her murmured comment, and immediately, in spite of her exhaustion, she busied herself with washing, brushing her hair, and changed her travel-stained dress for a fresh one.

Hardly had she finished when the door shook with a thunderous knock and immediately thereafter her brother burst in. He paused at the door, a huge, laughing, black-bearded giant, and stared at her. Then, saying only — "Nan!" — he

33

enveloped her in his great, powerful arms.

Nan could scarcely breathe. His rough shirt smelled of tobacco, of whiskey, of man sweat. Nan gasped. "Sam, Sam! Put me down, you fool! You'll crush me like an eggshell." But she was laughing — and crying, and suddenly the loss of her other brothers was dimmed, and this was like coming home.

Holding her beneath her arms, he dangled her before him at arms' length. "Nan! My God, you've grown up. You're a lady. Ah, Lordy, it's good to see you." He drew her close again, putting his scratchy, bearded lips down for a kiss.

When she could breathe again, she said in a small voice: "Sam, you're bigger . . . and stronger. And where did you get that beard? There'll be some changes made, friend Sam, and that beard will be the first to go."

He chuckled. "That's what I brought you out here for. To take over." He released her and stood back, big fists on hips, half laughing, half amazed. Nan colored at his close scrutiny, and Sam laughed uproariously at her discomfiture. "A lady! A grown-up lady! God Almighty, girl, how am I going to keep these woman-hungry miners away from you?"

"Who asked you to keep them away from me? They're men, aren't they?" Her eyes mocked him.

He laughed outright. "You're the same! You're the same old Nan!"

He fished a cigar from his pocket and bit off

the end. He fired it, puffed luxuriously, all this while studying her happily.

But there was that between them that could not be denied. She could see it in him, could feel it in herself. To take her mind from it, she asked: "What are you doing, Sam? Still looking for gold?"

This question brought it out, brought it into the open. He said soberly: "No, I'm forming a company of volunteers . . . cavalry. I'll take them East this winter and get into the fight. Nan, I want a payment on what they took from us at Bull Run." Sam's eyes had a bitter, bereaved look to them, a deep hurt.

Tears welled into Nan's eyes — tears because her brothers were gone, because they were never coming back. She sat down, thinking, openly weeping. Her voice was choked. "Sam, you should have seen them. They were like kids, proud of their new uniforms, shouting and ca-rousing, kissing their girls good bye like it was just another game they were playing. But it wasn't a game, Sam. It wasn't a game."

Sam came over and lifted her to her feet. His own eyes were suspiciously damp. And suddenly she was in his arms, her face against his hard-muscled chest, and he was patting her shoulder clumsily with a huge and hairy paw.

Chapter Four

With hands that trembled noticeably, Eames Jeffords poured himself another drink, downed it at a gulp, poured yet another. Murder writhed in his heart, and it was a full five minutes before he would trust himself to turn, to look across the lobby at Clee Fahr. Clee had changed. He was bigger, more solid. He still gave the same odd impression of steel under tension, although now to a much greater degree. *I could have killed him*, thought Jeffords, but there was no conviction in him. Clee had stood facing him, legs slightly parted, hands at his sides. Jeffords's own gun had been in his hand. Clee had made no move toward the Colt Navy revolver at his thigh, yet Jeffords had known that before he could clear his own gun and fire, that Clee's would be out, leveled, and firing.

I could have done it, thought Jeffords again and knew he lied. He watched Clee thumbing through the hotel register, uninterested for the most part in recent arrivals, but going back — going back. *Damn him!* Jeffords saw Clee halt, saw the abruptly increased tension in Clee, and knew by this instantly that Clee had come upon the name of Sibyl McAllister. Automatically Jeffords was calculating the distance to Clee, the probable consequences of shooting a man in the back in a crowded hotel lobby.

He saw Clee close the register with a bang and turn toward the stairway. Jeffords snapped his attention back to his drink and so entirely missed the look of pure venom Clee directed at him. When Jeffords looked again, Clee was almost to the top of the stairs.

First consciousness that others had witnessed his humiliation came as a voice spoke at his elbow, a heavy, familiar voice, rumbling out of a heavy man. "What the hell was all that about? He backed you up. What'd you let him do that for?"

Jeffords's face instantly lost its color. His eyes, as he turned, blazed white-hot rage, yet his voice was carefully held at its lowest pitch. "God damn you, Soames, don't question me. The man would have put a bullet into me before I could draw my gun."

The expression of Soames's face angered him. It was almost as though the thought aroused a certain pleasure in the man. Soames asked: "Who is he?"

"Clee Fahr."

"That's just a name. Who is he?"

Jeffords's face was that of a yellow-eyed Mephistopheles. Murder churned in his thoughts, this being very plain to the man who faced him. Yet Jeffords, ever honest with himself if with no one else, could admit that even in the presence of such an overpowering desire to kill he would never kill Clee Fahr in an open fight. Clee's skill must be counterbalanced by some other advantage for Jeffords. Clee must die, and Soames himself would agree, when he knew the story. For Clee had the knowledge that would make a farce of all Eames's careful planning. Clee could connect him with Sibyl.

There were other reasons why Jeffords wanted Clee dead. Personal reasons. For one thing, after the duel with Clee, he had been forced to flee. For another, he suspected, although he had never been able to make her admit it, that Clee occupied a prominent place in Sibyl's memory, and Jeffords could not tolerate competition, even that sort of competition. Soames was waiting for an answer to his question, and suddenly something about his expression stirred unreasoning anger in Jeffords. He gripped the edge of the bar, choking back the intemperate words that rose into his throat. *God damn Sibley, anyway! Why the hell did he have to send Soames with me? Why couldn't he let me do this job alone?* He knew the answer to that. Sibley didn't trust him. Sibley knew how he was with women, was afraid to trust him to keep out of scrapes.

Soames was waiting with exaggerated patience, and Jeffords said: "It goes back a long way. Before the war. I killed his cousin in a duel. He took it up, and I put him in the hospital." Soames's face mirrored disbelief. Before he could stop himself, Jeffords said defensively: "He's changed."

"He must have. What was the trouble about? A woman, I suppose?"

38

Jeffords nodded wearily. Soames was his equal in rank and could force a disclosure of all his relations with Clee.

"What woman?" It was as though Soames suspected what Jeffords's answer would be.

"Sibyl."

"God! He'll connect you with her." Soames was a big man. His heavy beard, the color of mud-laden water, had a way of concealing facial expressions, yet nothing could have concealed his present deep concern.

The murmur of talk along the bar worked its way into Eames Jeffords's mind as he waited for the words that would inevitably come from Soames. He almost grinned, for he knew what they would be.

The advent of Clee Fahr had stilled talk in the hotel bar, and all had closely watched the play between Fahr and Jeffords. Afterward, Jeffords knew, they had briefly discussed him, with little charity. Now, however, they were back at the same old subject, the Rebellion, as they chose to call the present conflict between the states.

Soames, his mind having masticated the problem thoroughly, now spoke the words Jeffords had known he would speak, the words Jeffords had been waiting for. "You'll have to get rid of him. We're too far along in this to let anything stop it, least of all one man who happens to hate you."

Jeffords tried to conceal his satisfaction. He made his protest sound sincere. "What if he does connect Sibyl with me? That was a personal thing and is all over. Sibyl's story is sound enough. Her home was threatened, so they sent her out here to live with her aunt and uncle. Ralph McAllister has been here since before the war. He's got a good claim on the Vasquez, and it keeps him busy. What is more natural than for Sibyl and her aunt to live here at the hotel?"

It was thin. Jeffords knew how thin it was. He knew it would not fool Clee, knew that Soames must also realize that it would not fool Clee.

"You'll have to quarrel with him," said Soames. "You'll have to fight him and kill him."

Jeffords laughed harshly. He bent close to Soames. "You fool!" he hissed. "Do you think I can kill him in a duel? What are you trying to do, get rid of me, so that all the glory for this mission will go to you? Or do you think I am afraid of him? Are you trying to make me admit it? Well, I will admit it." He watched Soames's eyes widen at his unexpected admission. Then he said: "I'm not afraid of him for personal reasons, and, if you doubt that, by God, I'll call you out. But how would it look to Sibley, if I were killed in a damned brawl over a woman? And how would you finish the job Sibley gave us to do, if I were dead and Sibyl discredited because gossip connected her with my death?"

Soames shrugged, but Jeffords could see that he had won. Soames said: "All right. I'll get Rogoff down from the mines. I'll get him to bring two or three others with him."

This was as Jeffords had wanted it. Yet he had not wanted to be the one to make the suggestion. He cautioned: "Fahr is tough."

Soames grinned. "So is Rogoff." He stepped away, down the length of the bar and into the street.

Eames Jeffords smiled his triumph, and tossed off his drink. He crossed the lobby and mounted the stairs. The tension of the evening had made him restless, and his swift pacing showed this restlessness plainly.

From the door of 112, across the hall from his own room, a man and woman emerged, the man a hairy giant of much the same cut as Soames, roughly dressed, black-bearded. But the woman. . . . Jeffords felt the old, hot, rising interest.

She was a tiny woman, her hair the gleaming black of polished ebony. Grace was, in her every movement, innocent provocation in her long-sweeping lashes, in the beautiful high-cheekboned face, in the deep blue eyes that brushed him briefly, went past, and returned with startled interest.

Eames Jeffords swept off his hat. His even teeth flashed a smile at her. He bowed slightly. Still the girl's glance lingered on him, in a puzzled way that was very flattering to Jeffords. He knew nothing of Nan's attraction to Clee, did not know she had watched the showdown between the two a few minutes before.

The giant growled — "Come on, Nan." — and

glared at Eames Jeffords. Jeffords gave the man his attention, recognized him, and nodded. "Good evening, Mister Massey."

He knew Massey for one of Denver City's more violent Unionists, was aware that Massey also knew him, knew his politics and his allegiance. Massey would have drawn the girl past, but the girl herself stopped him by saying: "Sam, don't be rude."

Massey made the introduction sourly. "Eames Jeffords, Miss Massey" — and could apparently not resist his further comment which was — "Jeffords is a Georgian, as you can tell from his talk. A disloyal man engaged in buying Union guns for the South."

Jeffords shrugged, smiling, and murmured: "A man follows his conscience." He managed to bring a practiced gleam of patriotic zeal to his eyes.

Nan Massey nodded pleasantly and gave Jeffords her hand. The interested speculation in her eyes excited him, and his glance turned bold. Nan Massey discreetly lowered her eyes and had the grace to blush.

Sam Massey dragged her away impatiently, his voice rumbling unintelligibly in her ear. Jeffords watched them, smiling, wondering if he had shown the boldness too soon, if it had frightened her.

He waited as they turned at the head of the stairs for the girl's backflung glance. When she did not turn, his smile widened. No. He had not frightened her, or she would have been unable to resist another look at him. He thought: *This one will be interesting. This one will be very much worthwhile.* He opened the door and went into his room.

Sibyl McAllister was a tall woman, nearly as tall as Eames Jeffords. Her hair tonight was piled high upon her stately head, a mound of red-bronze that served only to accentuate the pure whiteness of her skin, the gray-green fire of her eyes. Her mouth was a splash of scarlet, thinned a little, twisted as she looked at Eames Jeffords.

God, how I hate him! she thought, yet, as he turned from the door, she could feel herself melting, could feel the fire that was born in the depths of her body growing, searing, leaping high until its flame burned unbidden in her eyes. Her long legs turned weak as he looked at her. Her beasts rose and fell in increasing cadence. *Damn him! Damn him! Damn him!*

"What are you doing here?" he asked harshly.

She was silent, showing him the naked hate burning in her eyes, burning and rising from the same bed of coals that nurtured her passion.

He laughed. "All right. Later. Do you know who came in on the stage tonight?"

"Who?" Her voice was choked, almost a cry of pain. She didn't care right now if Jefferson Davis himself had come in on the stage. She wanted Jeffords, and he damned well knew she did. Yet he would torment her for an hour with polite and pointless conversation, teasing, pretending

43

he did not see what was so plainly obvious in her eyes. She realized that her hands were shaking, and she clasped them tightly together.

Jeffords was smiling, smiling in a peculiar, mocking way. He said: "Clee Fahr."

Instantly Sibyl chilled. It was as though ice water had been thrown upon the fires that were consuming her. Her voice was a whisper. "What does he want?"

"How the hell should I know what he wants? I know he'll make trouble for us. I know that much. He'll make trouble, unless I kill him."

Sibyl's instinct was to cry out, to protest, even to beg. She halted herself in time, hoped she had prevented her concern from showing in her face. She asked, letting concern now show plainly in her voice: "Did he see you?"

He nodded, and Sibyl noted the strange glow in his eyes. He said: "He'll connect you with me. He'll think you're here with me. So I'll kill him."

Sibyl knew what he was doing now. He somehow suspected that she still cherished some feeling for Clee. She thought: *No. You'll never kill Clee. You're not man enough, and you never will be.* She was remembering Clee, tall and loose and easily smiling, yet so filled with unpredictable wildness. From the first, Clee had been the one she wanted. It was her own fault, she could realize now, that Clee had held back in favor of Darrel, yet she was aware as well that it is woman's way to show less warmth to the favored one. This she had done, and this had lost her both Darrel and Clee, and given her instead this . . . this. . . . Suddenly she did not even want to talk to Jeffords, could not stand the sight of him. She concealed her growing revulsion, saying only: "I'll be going, Eames." She moved toward the door.

Jeffords smiled, his eyes mocking. "Have you forgotten so soon what you came here for?"

Sibyl turned. Her voice was low, yet vibrant with passion. "I ought to kill you, Eames! I ought to have killed you a long time ago. Someday I'll do it."

Jeffords laughed with pure delight. Interest and desire which she had been unable to kindle with her passion, she now kindled easily with her rage. He made a step toward her, but she opened the door and fled into the hall.

Sibyl opened her door and went into the rooms she shared with her aunt. They were entirely dark, and her aunt was sleeping noisily, a great mound of flesh on the bed. Soft moonlight filtered through the window and laid its unearthly pattern on the floor.

Sibyl walked to the window and stared down into the street. The expression on her beautiful face was exceedingly soft, for she was remembering Clee, his strength, his wildness, his gentleness, the smoky color of his eyes. Her lips parted, and she moistened them with the tip of her tongue.

She slipped out of her clothes, stretched, reveled in the caress of moonlight upon her naked body. Like the touch of hands — Clee's hands. She smiled lightly. Yet as she slipped carefully between the sheets, a single caution impressed itself upon her. *I must never let him see how much I hate Eames, for if I do, he will begin to suspect. He will know that so much hate cannot live without something to feed itself upon.*

Chapter Five

On the morning of August 27, 1861, Sam Massey, having installed Nanette in a comfortable, if small, log cabin on Cherry Creek between Denver and the Platte, saddled his horse for the ride to the mines. Clee Fahr rode into the cabin clearing just as Sam was mounting. This morning, Clee was attired in citizen's clothes, yet he clung to his boots, to the wide-brimmed, black cavalry hat. And he had discarded neither the .36-caliber Colt revolver nor the short, bone-handled knife.

He could not have said exactly why he had ridden this way today. He knew that his mind was disturbed by the increasing necessity of taking either one side or the other in the conflict. He knew, as well, that in his present state of uneasiness his thoughts were prone to remember Nanette Massey with increasing regularity. There had been so much serenity about her, so much smiling pleasure. He had not known the exact location of the Massey cabin and considered himself fortunate to have found it so easily.

He swept off his hat and advanced, grinning easily. Massey looked at him uncertainly, but Nanette smiled a genuine welcome. Interest and warmth flared in her eyes. She said: "Sam, this is Cletus Fahr. He rode up on the stage with me from Bent's Fort to Denver." Her eyes twinkled and teased as she looked at Clee, and he could feel the color seeping into his face. It was plain enough to him that Nanette's thoughts were on the incident at the way station.

Massey was scowling, sensing some by-play between them, not understanding it. He seemed reluctant to leave.

Nanette asked: "Where are you bound for, Mister Fahr?"

"Seeing the country."

She brightened. "Why don't you ride with Sam? He's headed for the Vasquez." She seemed pleased at the prospect of giving Clee and her brother this excellent opportunity of becoming acquainted.

Massey grunted, leaned down, and gave her a light kiss.

Clee said: "If you don't mind . . . ?"

"Sure not. Come on."

Clee touched his hat brim, and the two rode off, splashed across Cherry Creek, and disappeared into the grove of cottonwoods that lined its twisting bank. Clee grinned wryly. "Your sister is a beautiful woman." He would rather have stayed, would rather have spent a pleasant hour with Nanette. She had wished it otherwise.

Clee's compliment softened Massey's grim taciturnity. He grinned. "Damned if she ain't. She's growed up some since I last saw her."

Clee asked: "Do you have a claim on the Vasquez?"

"Uhn-huh. Such as it is. Pays me good wages, when I work it. No more than that." He had been watching Clee, showing some puzzlement, showing some natural reserve. Suddenly, as though he had come to some decision, the reserve went out of him, and he grinned, a huge and carefree grin that gave his approval of Clee and showed his liking. "I'm not fooling with it now. I've been organizing a company of Volunteers. I'm headed for the Vasquez today to bring them to Denver."

"You expect to see action in Colorado?"

Massey shrugged. "I won't be here. I'm taking the company East." He hesitated. "I lost three brothers killed and one captured at Bull Run. I reckon I owe the Johnny Reb something for that." He stared hard at Clee. "You a Union man?"

Clee said — "Massachusetts." — and wondered why he felt like a liar.

Surprise showed in the big man's eyes. "You don't look it." He hesitated for just a moment, and then drew his horse close and stuck out his hand. "Indiana."

Clee liked his firm grip, his honest eyes. He said: "I've been in the West for several years, trapping and prospecting. I just came up here from my cousin's place in Texas." He noted the instant reserve that came over Massey, the coolness, and said quite frankly: "It's black and white for most men. It isn't quite that way for me. I was born in Massachusetts, but one of my uncles

49

lived in Georgia, and I visited there a lot. It's easy enough to say that slavery is wrong, but I think the North has chosen the wrong way to correct the wrong."

Massey frowned. "Hell, I can't see that. Men ain't supposed to be owned . . . bought and sold like cattle."

"I agree with that. Yet to the Southerners, they are property, honestly bought and paid for according to law."

"I'm damned if I see your point."

They had entered the road, and now turned westward. Scorning the ferry, they splashed their horses across the shallow breadth of the Platte.

Clee grinned as they climbed the steep, opposite bank. He said: "Supposing you owned a dozen horses. Suppose you used them and needed them to work your farm in Indiana. Suppose that, when you bought them, it was perfectly legal and right for you to do so. Then along comes the government in Washington and says . . . 'Here, Massey, we've decided it's wrong to own horses. Up here, we use mules to farm.' So they make you turn your horses loose."

"Hell, man, that's silly. Men and horses ain't the same."

"But the principle is. You bought the horses and paid good hard money for them. You violated no law in doing it. You need the horses to farm your land. And then along comes somebody and lays down the order to let them go."

Massey scratched his head.

Clee pressed his advantage. "Besides that, a planter in the South pays a thousand, two thousand dollars for a slave. It isn't unusual for a man to have a dozen. Some have a hundred or more. If you had a dozen, you'd have fifteen or twenty thousand dollars tied up in them. Would you let the government arbitrarily take that much money away from you?"

"Hell, no, I wouldn't." Massey grinned uncomfortably. "You sure got me in a corner that time."

For a long time they rode in silence, across broad, rolling lands, knee deep in grass. The mountains loomed ahead of them, and they entered the foothills, with Sam Massey frowning at his thoughts. Finally he said: "All right. Suppose the government is wrong. You can't go on keeping slaves forever. All the rest of the civilized world has abolished slavery. What do you say about that?"

"I didn't say it was wrong to abolish slavery. It isn't. It is only the method that is wrong. What do you think would happen, if they turned the thousands of slaves in the South loose all at once?" He felt himself warming to his subject and grinned wryly.

Massey considered his question for a moment, then said: "Why, I reckon all hell would break loose."

Clee nodded. "It would. Most of them can't read or write. They have always had shelter and their meals and clothing provided for them.

51

They know nothing but work in the fields. Where would they go? What would they do?"

"Hell, now you're getting me all mixed up. You got it figured out how it should be done?"

"I've thought about it some. I think the government should go at it slowly. They should say that all Negro children under the age of ten, and those born thereafter, are free. That would create no particular problem, would occasion no actual loss to the planters. They should establish schools for these children and see that they are educated."

"What then?"

"Free the others gradually, by age groups, after first paying their owners a fair and reasonable price for them. Take them under the right of Eminent Domain, the rights of government to seize private property for the public good. Educate them. Prepare them for the life of free men. Taking them in this way would work no hardship on the planters, no hardship too serious to be overcome. It would not upset the South's economy."

"Hell, that kind of a system would take years."

"What of it? Do you think this war is going to take less time? Do you think this war will cost less than paying for the slaves would cost? And, besides the dollar cost, this war is costing in lives."

Massey stared at Clee with genuine respect. "Why didn't somebody think of that before they started fighting?"

Clee shrugged, then said bitterly: "Because there are fortunes to be made out of war. Because there is no money to be made from charity and humanity."

"You think this war is right? You think a state should be able to cut loose from the Union every time they disagree with some law that's passed? You think it was right for the South to fire on Fort Sumter?"

"No, I guess not. Hell, man, I don't know."

"Which side are you on?" Massey's question was blunt. "You can't straddle the fence forever. What you going to do if they call you for the Army?"

Clee shrugged wearily. He knew Massey was right. He had to get off the fence sometime. But it went against his grain to fight against either South or North. Most men had resolved their doubts the easy way. They had blindly espoused the side under whose protection they happened to have been born. Yet Clee had never been a man to choose the easy way. Again, incomprehensibly, he recalled that drunken Texan at the dirty bar in Paradero, recalled the boasting talk. On impulse, he asked: "Would you take your company East if you knew the Confederacy was planning to take Colorado?"

Massey's eyes widened. His mouth was slack for a moment, showing his utter surprise. Then his eyes narrowed. "And how would you know a thing like that, bucko?"

Clee realized suddenly that the time had come

for a decision. It seemed rather odd to him that the time should come today, in this way, because of an entirely impulsive remark. Now, if he amplified his statement regarding the Confederate plan, he would be irrevocably lined up with the Union. On the other hand, he could still pass it off as something of no import. He made the decision, when he said: "There was a Confederate captain in a bar in Paradero. He was drunk and wanted to brag. Maybe I egged him on a little." The sense of being right was increasing in him. He thought of Eames Jeffords, but he looked at Massey, unconsciously comparing the two. The comparison was unfair, as he well knew. You cannot compare two systems as easily as you compare two individuals. He admitted at last that only one thing had eventually decided him. No man fights against the land of his birth. It was that simple. He felt a vast relief. He said: "The man was about as drunk as he could get. He might not have been telling the truth, but he said the Confederacy intended to take Colorado."

"Man, the governor ought to hear this."

Clee shrugged. "Maybe. Maybe he already knows it."

"What makes you think they'd bother with Colorado?"

"Why not? What are they going to run short of first?"

"Why, guns I reckon. Powder and ball. Railroad equipment."

Unnoticed by either, they had passed the

Mount Vernon House, had entered the long and winding Apex Cañon. Here the way was rocky and narrow, and the shod hoofs of their horses rang and clattered and echoed from the high hills on either side. Great, yellow pines, long-leafed and dense, their trunks four feet thick, stood like sentinels beside the road. Clee said: "They'll be short of all kinds of manufactured articles, for the South has no factories. They will have to buy these things abroad, and they'll need gold to buy them. Where are they going to get the gold after what they have is gone?"

Sam Massey whistled. "Colorado. And after that, California."

"That's what I've been thinking. But down in Texas, General Sibley is short of guns, short of supplies, short of artillery, short of everything, in fact, but men. He's got three or four thousand men, guns and ammunition for only part of them. He needs horses and mules and a lot of supplies before he can threaten Colorado."

Massey laughed. "Then what the hell are we worrying about? The Confederacy won't give him those things. They're busy enough at home."

"A quarter of a million in gold would buy Sibley what he needs."

"Man, you're crazy. Where would he git it . . . in Texas?"

Clee drew his horse to a halt, facing Massey. He asked: "How much comes out of these mines on the Vasquez every month?"

Sam shrugged. "I don't know. A hundred thousand maybe."

"What do they do with it?"

"There's a safe in the stageline's office in Denver. Whenever they think they've got enough accumulated, they send it out on. . . ." For an instant Massey's huge, bearded face was like carved granite.

Clee grinned at him. "One shipment would be a good start for Sibley, wouldn't it?"

"Clee, you're crazy! You're crazy!"

"Maybe. But if I'm not, you'll miss a lot of action by going East."

Doubt stirred in Massey's eyes. "Well, the boys are kind of set on it. They wouldn't stay unless they were pretty sure of seeing a fight."

Clee remained silent as their horses rose through the thickly wooded, rocky hills. He was reminded by the smell of hot pine resin of the South again, of Georgia. He wondered briefly why he had not seen Sibyl during the two days of his stay at the Fremont House, why he had continued to rely on a chance encounter, why he had not taken the bit between his teeth and sought her out. He knew the answer to that one without too much puzzling. He had not been sure he wanted to renew the feelings he'd had for Sibyl.

Massey asked now: "My God, do you think they'd rob the safe in the stageline office?"

"Maybe not the office. I think they will rob the stage. I think that Jeffords is buying guns to equip a force of some kind. When he gets them armed, when he finds out which stage is taking out the gold. . . ." He shrugged. "He'll take stage and all. He'll take the men that did the job south to join up with Sibley. They'll raid ranches all the way to Texas, and by the time they get there they'll be driving a thousand horses and mules ahead of them. Then, my friend, you and your troop will get all the action you want. You'll get all you can hold and a lot more besides."

At Cresswell they halted, unsaddled, and had a late dinner of elk steaks and fried potatoes. In late afternoon they dropped down the long and twisting shelf road to the clear, tumbling Vasquez, turned left along the stream, and shortly came into the collection of shacks and tents, the haphazard collection of hastily constructed shelters which was dignified by the name of Idaho.

At this time of day, the miners were quitting work, tramping in a long line from upcreek and down, making their common destination the huge saloon tents in the center of the settlement, the gambling halls, the smoky restaurants. Pleasure, in Idaho, relegated to itself no particular time of day. Saloons ran twenty-four hours, and at all hours of day and night could be heard the shrill laughter of the camp's few women, busy, never quite satisfying the demand for their services.

A damned hole, thought Clee, *a damned boar's nest,* yet even to Clee the atmosphere of the camp was exciting, for the spirit of the camp was the spirit of the men in it, adventurous, carefree, rowdy, drunken. Heavy beards were the rule, sobriety the exception. After a long day at sluicebox and pan, every man's effort seemed to be concentrated upon getting as drunk as possible, as quickly as possible. As they rode down the narrow, muddy street, they were halted momentarily by two miners, fighting savagely with fists and knees. Farther down, a volley of shots echoed from within one of the saloon tents.

Sam Massey laughed aloud. "I'll give you two to one that's them."

Clee, at the man's odd tone, looked at him, surprising a gleam of pure, savage joy on the big man's heavily bearded face.

Massey's blue eyes glowed. He glanced at Clee, grinned wryly, then said: "They're a ragged outfit. They don't give a damn except for three things . . . a bottle, a woman, and a fight."

As though to bear out his remark, the tent front suddenly erupted in a half a hundred shouting, laughing, and drunken men. Some of them carried revolvers or rifles, the others bottles, chairs, or clubs. Just beyond the tent from which they had come, the town ended, and there began the wide-scattered shacks and tents of the miners. There also, in a small clearing, were the miners' fires, a couple of dozen of them, kindled in this single clearing from the common need for comradeship and company.

Into this clearing they boiled, shooting, shouting, stumbling, and falling. Suddenly one of them seized a piece of flaming wood from one of the fires and, with a howl of demoniacal glee, hurled it high into the air. In the gathering dusk, it made a glowing, flaming parabola, landing amidst a dozen men who howled and jumped and beat at their flaming clothes with their hands. The man who had flung it, his imagination aroused, howled: "Sumter! Give 'em hell, Yanks!"

Immediately the group split in two, as quickly as though at a sharp command. Half rushed to the group among which had been flung the firebrand, the other half quickly taking the side of the man who had flung it. As they ran, they snatched burning sticks from the fires and, yelling, flung them into the air.

On the Rebel side a man screeched: "Whip the god-damned Abolitionists! Give 'em hell! Charge! Charge! We'll give 'em Bull Runs till they can't stand up!"

From the other side, another bawled: "Whip the Secesh, by God! Whip 'em! Whip 'em! Whip the god-damned pants off 'em! Charge!"

Clee, grinning, looked at Sam. Sam was doubled over in his saddle, face red, choking. One of the firebrands, flung harder than the rest, landed atop the saloon tent, and in an instant the whole thing was ablaze. The front of it emptied screaming and scantily clad women, cursing miners, and a saloon-keeper who was beside himself with rage. He was a small man, sour of face, bald as a freshly laid egg. His face was purple, and he hopped, first on one leg, then on the other, meanwhile screeching: "Gott tamn! Gott tamn! Fire!"

Massey made a gurgling sound and rolled from his horse. The horse moved away, leaving huge Sam Massey on the ground, hugging his heaving and straining sides. Tears streamed into the man's black beard.

Like a miniature artillery duel the battle raged, firebrands making their flaming patterns against the somber hills and the darkening sky. The creek tumbled its tireless, tinkling way toward the plain. The camp ceased all activity, save for that of keeping the blaze from spreading, and came to watch. Shirts disappeared from the combatants' hairy chests, torn away by the force of their savage grappling.

At last there weren't two sides, but only one huge pile of fighting, cursing, and kicking men. Gradually, gradually the enthusiasm slacked off, and here and there a man rose, laughing, angry, quickly sobering, panting, swearing, and blackened by the fire ashes on the ground. Massey got up, spent and weary from his laughing. He walked over and caught his horse. One of the brawlers spied him, and at once the shout went up. "Massey! Here's Cap'n Massey, boys!"

As though at a signal, the fight broke up, and the whole crowd shuffled toward Clee and Sam, shame-faced and grinning.

Their leader made a sloppy and perfunctory salute. "All present 'n' 'counted for, Cap'n. When do we leave?"

Hard eyes — reckless faces. Young faces, savage, carefree, fighting faces. Muscles hardened and turning stringy by toil, by danger's daily companionship. Clee thought: *God! Give Massey a thousand like these and God help Sibley's Rebels!*

Chapter Six

Morning, an autumn morning on the Vasquez, came cold and chill. A light, hoary frost lay over the grass. High on the hillsides, amid the deep, somber green of the pines, there showed an occasional patch of lighter aspen, and here and there among their leaves a spot of gleaming, yellow gold. A mist rose from the river, a fine, gray mist that mingled with campfire smoke and became the color of Cletus Fahr's humorous eyes. Even before the sun touched the tips of the peaks with its shining light, the camp was fully astir. Clee, astride his horse, shivered, for his clothes were not meant for this altitude, this cold, and his blood had been thinned by the summer heat of Texas.

Down through the light and scattered brush that lined the riverbank marched the company, eighty-seven men, in ragged formation, a murderous crew looking not at all like soldiers in the Union Army. Before them and off to one side strode their sergeant, O'Rourke, a giant of a man, fully six feet four, bearded as were most of the others, raggedly and roughly dressed.

"Squads right!" he roared, and patiently waited for the mess to unscramble. "Halt! Fo'ward, hwup! Squads left! At the double, hwup!" Running, a bunched and disorderly column, they came directly toward the small clearing where Clee and Massey and the company's lieutenant, Curt Champion, sat their fidgeting horses.

Massey began to chuckle as they drew near. Clee glanced at him, saw the glow of irrepressible merriment in his eyes.

Champion grinned. "What the hell have you cooked up now, Sam?"

"Wait." He began to laugh silently. "Just keep watchin'."

Clee began to grin expectantly. Was there no end to the pranking of these pseudo-soldiers? Whatever this was, it was sure to be good.

"Column right . . . !" The executing command was slow in coming for to the right of the column lay a solid screen of brush. "Hwup!"

The column turned, running into a narrow break in the trees, a break where light, low brush concealed the ground. Massey began to laugh with soft delight. The leaders of the column went down like pins in a bowling alley. Those behind them, running blindly, piled up on top. The column's rear halted, but the sergeant bawled: "Now who in the hell said halt? Just because those damned clumsy bastards in front can't keep their feet is no reason . . . !"

The column plowed on. Curt Champion began to grin reluctantly. The sergeant bawled: "The Rebs are right behind you, boys. Run, dammit, run!"

Suddenly the column stopped. A low growl of

outrage rose from the men on the ground as they scrambled to their feet. They started for the sergeant, and he backed away saying placatingly: "Now, boys. Now, boys."

They were on him with a rush. By legs and arms, with little gentleness, they carried him, loudly protesting, vainly remonstrating, to the bank of the icy creek. "One, two" — the count came simultaneously in four score throats — "three!"

The sergeant described a slow, gentle arc from the bank. He landed with a monstrous splash in the icy water, thrashed about for a moment, then came dripping and gasping to his feet. For the briefest instant rage darkened his broad, flat features, then a grin began to form behind his eyes.

Tears streamed down Massey's face. Champion was openly laughing, yet he could say through his laughter: "Sam, how the hell you going to get any discipline out of them when you pull stunts like that?"

One of the men now drew his knife and, walking back to the spot where the company had piled up, cut loose the rope that had been stretched tightly between two trees, six inches from the ground.

Massey growled incoherently, but with complete conviction: "Discipline be damned! Wait till you see them fight!"

He rode toward them, with Clee and Champion a little behind. His roaring, huge voice carried half a mile. "All right! Break it up! The review's over. Start 'em out for Denver, Sergeant."

At once there was a rumbling, growing sound among the ranks. It swelled and roared back from the surrounding hills in a reverberating echo. O'Rourke's bellow was ignored in the confusion, yet to Clee's amazed eyes order seemed to come magically from chaos. Those who owned horses got them swiftly and mounted, then formed a curveting, variable column of twos. The men without mounts marched away on the road toward Denver to the accompaniment of a bawdy song.

Armed to the teeth they were, revolvers slung from their hips or thrust into the waistband of their pants. Long knives dangled from sheaths. Rifles, and an occasional cavalry saber, waved in the air.

Along the single street of Idaho the crowd stood three deep, saloon-keepers, bottle-waving miners, and women with painted faces. In the eyes of some of the women tears glistened, and the men shouted: "Give 'em hell, boys. Give the damned Johnny Reb somethin' for Bull Run!"

Massey, followed closely by Champion and Clee, spurred his horse and thundered to the head of the column. And so, in early dusk on August 28, 1861, F Company of the first regiment of Colorado Volunteers marched into Denver.

In late afternoon of September 1st, a cold wind stirred in the north, rushed down across the limitless plain, driving before it low, scudding, slate-gray clouds. By nightfall, the clouds began to condense into fine, driving rain, rain that could chill a man in minutes, rain that turned the deep dust of the streets to slippery, clinging mud. Clee Fahr, a cloak billowing about his hickory-tough body, stamped the mud from his feet at the entrance to the Fremont House at seven and strode inside.

Shock, worse than a blow, stopped him in his tracks before he was halfway across the deeply carpeted lobby, for Sibyl was descending the stairs, glorious as a vision in a velvet gown of deep blue, her eyes fixed upon him with a curious, pleading intensity. Naked eyes, defenseless eyes.

Hat in hand, he waited at the foot of the stairs, waited while she ran the last few steps and flung herself into his arms. "'Clee! Clee!" It was a cry that swept away instantly the barrier of the years. It was a cry that blotted out hate, and murder, and desire for revenge.

His hands were like claws in the soft flesh of her arms. He held her away, an almost savage expression in his face. The gown was low-cut, revealing more of her full and upthrust breasts than it concealed.

"Clee," she said, ignoring that savagery in his face. "Clee, where have you been? What have you been doing? Oh, it's been so long . . . so very long."

He had been a lonely man for all these years,

carrying with him in his mind a vision of the perfection that was Sibyl McAllister. Suddenly this dream of perfection was reality, and in his arms. Suddenly Sibyl was no cold, distant dream, but warmth, and urgent pressure, and eyes that pleaded for more than this embrace under the glance of a dozen lobby loungers.

Her face was fragile, alive, vibrant. Her eyes were green-gray, startling eyes that stopped a man with a shock whenever he looked into them. Her skin was smooth, cream-velvet, delicately tinted with pink on her cheeks, tinted with the pink of pleasure and joy. Yet some nameless thing intruded between them, a feeling, an instinct that would not ignore the coincidence of Sibyl's presence here simultaneously with that of Eames Jeffords.

Clee's voice was harsh. "Have you had your dinner?"

She shook her head wordlessly, her eyes caressing his face.

"Then have it with me. Not here. There's a place . . . ," he broke off, knowing before he looked that the man now descending the stairs was Eames Jeffords. There was a certain coldness in Clee's spine, a certain prickle at the back of his neck. As though from some ancient, savage prompting, his hackles sought to rise.

Jeffords gave him a smooth, sardonic smile, touched his hat coldly to Sibyl. Clee watched Jeffords until the man went into the bar, then returned his attention to Sibyl.

The glance she gave him was abject. "Clee, that is done. Please, please don't stir it up again."

He shrugged. "I tried that the night I arrived, and failed. If there is any stirring done now, it will have to be Eames that does it. Get your coat."

Unmoving, he watched her ascent of the stairs. When she had disappeared from sight, he took a cigar absently from his pocket, bit off the end, and lighted it. His face was singularly cold; his eyes were a deep, slate-gray.

She returned, hurrying lightly, desperately trying to conceal her nervousness, her fear at Clee's coldness. He handed her up into a carriage, rising immediately to the seat beside her. She was soft and warm beside him, and her fragrance was a subtle, elusive scent of magnolia, a scent that could stir in him at once all of the old memories and hungers, all of the old violence.

Had his brain not been filled with Sibyl, with his need for her and his tortured doubt of her, he might have seen the three men who sheltered themselves from the rain in a doorway ten yards up the street. As it was, caution, usually such a vital part of him, was stilled tonight, and he rode through the dripping air with everything driven from his thoughts but the breathtaking beauty of this woman beside him.

Nick Rogoff stood but a short five feet four. He waited tonight, half obscured by darkness, with a cloak about his shoulders that reached nearly to the ground. As the carriage splashed past, he spoke shortly to one of the men beside him. "Get your horse. See where he goes. But no trouble, you understand? No trouble while she is with him."

The man faded into the rain, and an instant later the sound of a horse, running in mud, receded into the night. Rogoff seemed to drift deeper into the shelter of the doorway, and then a match flared, briefly illuminating his face as he touched the flame to the tip of a cigar.

His was a broad, flat-featured face, strong of jaw, wide of forehead. His cheeks were adorned with graying sideburns, his upper lip with a long mustache that almost entirely hid his thin, cruel mouth. His face was not an evil one, until you saw his eyes, until you caught their pale, ice-green color, their utter ruthlessness, and entire lack of feeling. Even in the cold heart of Eames Jeffords, this man could stir a kind of uneasy terror, for Rogoff was not a fighter. He was an assassin, who, for pay or personal satisfaction, could kill a man or woman with less feeling than Jeffords would experience over shooting a prairie rattler. He could wait, and did tonight, with patience that approached serenity. He was a cat at a chipmunk burrow, knowing that the reward for patience is success, knowing this because it had always been so before.

Half an hour passed. A horseman came then, slowly trotting through the mire to pause before the darkened doorway. "He went to the Planter's

House, Nick. What now?"

"He'll be back. He'll probably leave the woman off and return uptown on this side of the street. But we'll be sure of him. Go on down the street. Do you see that old corral? Stand inside it behind one of the posts. Rest your rifle on the corral poles. If he comes your way, wait until he steps into the light from the Fremont House dining room, then shoot."

The man clucked to his horse and splashed away. The man in the doorway with Rogoff shivered. Rogoff spoke to him without turning. "Go upstreet to the corner. Let him come by. Let him take the woman into the hotel. But do not let him pass you a second time. If he should cross the street, instead of passing me, he's your man. Do you understand?"

"Sure. All right." The man shuffled away, grumbling.

Rogoff caught enough of his words to get the gist of complaint. He did not like ambushing a man. Rogoff determined instantly not to let Clee get past this doorway. He felt contempt for men whose sensibilities balked at a simple job like this one. He wondered about the man he had sent downstreet, wondered if he could be trusted to carry out his orders.

In the end, success or failure in this depended on Rogoff himself. Softly, silently the minutes ticked away. Another hour passed. At last the carriage returned, and Clee handed Sibyl McAllister down to the plank walk. They stood for a moment, close in the misting rain. Her face was uptilted, a pale and lovely oval, and her words reached Rogoff as a whisper. "Clee, come up for a while. Aunt is gone to the Vasquez overnight. Clee, please."

"No." The word seemed torn from Clee. "I've got to think."

"Later, Clee?"

"Maybe." Almost roughly, he drew her up the two short steps to the hotel door. She passed inside with but a pale and pleasing smile. Then Clee turned back to the street, hunched slightly against the rain, scowling.

The carriage driver spoke to him, and Clee handed up some money. After that, the carriage splashed down the street toward the river.

Rogoff moved ever so slightly. His long cloak stirred as his hand went under it and closed itself over the heavy, walnut pistol grips. Still he waited. The saloons and the town's gaiety were uptown, and an uptown course would bring Clee directly past Rogoff's doorway. Nothing lay downstreet, nothing but a few corrals, an Indian camp, and the winding bottom of Cherry Creek.

Yet it was downstreet that Clee turned, and Rogoff rumbled a low curse beneath his breath, immediately moving out into the rain and taking to the walk behind Clee at a fast and almost silent trot.

In the Fremont House bar, Eames Jeffords saw Sibyl come in and go thoughtfully and slowly up the stairs. With an almost painful anticipation he waited for the shots that he knew were sure to come.

Immediately as he turned downstreet, a vague and troubled wariness hit Clee. There was no sound in the street save for the *drip-drip* of rain from the eaves of the hotel verandah, the retreating sound of the carriage, the distant, hushed sound of the merrymaking along McGaa, and the faint howl of the wind through the cottonwoods that lined the banks of Cherry Creek. Yet it was as though he had heard the click of a thumbed-back hammer, the cocking of a dry-gulcher's rifle. This feeling was that quick, but certain.

An odd chill raced down Clee's spine. This, then, was the way Jeffords would strike. Clee's ears strained. He stepped lightly on the balls of his feet, making no sound. Every nerve and muscle in his body was taut to the point where it seemed that any additional strain would snap him. His eyes probed the shadows to right and left as he controlled the impulse that seized him to run, to dive aside. *Not yet. Not yet.* Before him suddenly lay the square of light that was cast on the walk and street from the bright, crystal chandeliers in the hotel dining room. Instinct warned him that here, if anywhere, lay the danger. Yet without pausing, he stepped directly into this soft glow of light. As he did so, he caught the faintest stir in the darkness from the corral across the street, the slightest of movements, apparently, but a thickening of one of the corral posts, and at almost the same instant heard the soft slap of running feet behind him.

Clee Fahr needed no thought now to tell him that this was an ambush, an extraordinarily well-planned and deadly one. Nor was there any lag in time between his hearing and seeing, and the action those sounds and sights conceived. He was flat on the walk, rolling, when the bullet tore into the hotel window behind him. He was on his knees, turning, gun in hand, as Rogoff came pounding toward him.

Again the discharging rifle, muffled and vicious, came from across the street. Something slammed its savage force against Clee's shoulder, and his gun skittered across the wet and slippery walk. A man yelled — "Again! Again!" — and instantly then the squat, short figure, approaching him, veered into the street, away from the light and the front of the hotel which must soon be crowded with the curious.

Now, immediately, a revolver bloomed in the pitch black that shrouded the muddy street. But Clee was up, running, crouching. This slug tore a hole in his calf, missing the bone, but instantly crippling him. He fell, rolled off the walk, and into the street.

Miraculously, he came out of the pitiless, revealing light with this motion, and now, in darkness with both guns spitting at him frantically, he hobbled the endless twenty yards to the hotel hitch rack farther downstreet.

Three or four horses stood there, soaked and miserable, but roused from their head-down apathy by the turmoil of shouts and shots. Clinging to the rail, unarmed, Clee fumbled with the knotted reins of the closest one, a black with a gleaming, streaming hide. The shots ceased, and the street mud made a sucking, clinging sound as the running footsteps approached. Clee heard the hissing words: "Fool! Fool! One shot should have done it!"

It was Clee's right calf which had been penetrated by the revolver bullet. He slammed his left foot into the stirrup, holding his weight against the nervous animal's side by the strength of his right arm. The horse whirled away into the street, with Clee clinging to him this way.

Again the flaming gun muzzle flashed from behind. The black faltered, stumbled, and almost fell. Clee used his recovering surge to hoist himself into the saddle, and then, half bucking, half running, the horse raced down the street.

Nausea and overpowering weakness rose like a tide from Clee's pain-racked body, flooding his thoughts and his brain, killing his will, nearly killing his consciousness. He did not know where he was going, only that those who would kill him were close behind and that he was unarmed. He entered the thicket that lined the north bank of Cherry Creek and pounded away toward the west.

Chapter Seven

Within a short quarter mile, the dripping brush had soaked Clee thoroughly. His senses reeled. All of his concentration was centered upon staying on the back of this plunging, frightened, and wounded horse, thus leaving him little thought for the shouts, muted by increasing distance, behind him. He had been headed for the small cabin of the Masseys earlier when he had turned downstreet instead of up as Rogoff had expected. He could realize now that only this had saved his life.

Without checking his horse's mad flight, he now remembered his destination. What right had he to lead a pack of killers to Sam Massey's cabin? Yet reason told him: *You're bleeding. If you don't get help soon, you're finished.*

There was no help for it then. He let the horse have his head, guiding him only perfunctorily in the general direction of the cabin, refusing to let him leave the shelter of these trees. He began to chill. The wind howled mercilessly against him, cold, bitter, and he began to shiver violently. His pursuers, forced to follow tracks, continued to drop behind, until their shouts were entirely lost in the whistling wind.

Yet, of this Clee was sure. They would track their wounded quarry until they found him.

That was inevitable. And if Clee did not have help, if he did not some way get dry and warm and have the flow of blood from his wounds stanched, he would be dead when they did find him.

Where the cottonwood timber began to thin before the Masseys' clearing, Clee tied the reins to the saddle horn and let himself roll from it. The horse, well-trained, slowed. But the terror of this night, the smell of blood, and the pain of the animal's wound overcame his training and after a short, initial hesitation, he resumed his headlong flight.

Clee, flat on the wet, sandy ground, could not even feel elated at this. Instead, he crawled along until his hand closed over a wet, knobby cottonwood branch. He broke it off to the right length while still on the ground, then, rising and using the stick for a cane, hobbled in the direction of the cabin.

Rain pounded harder against him. The creek, swelled by runoff, made a low murmur, audible even above the howl of the wind. After an eternity of painful hobbling, Clee caught a glimpse of a faint square of light and knew instantly that it was fire glow from the cabin's window. Sam and his sister had retired then, and this light was the glow from a dying fire on the hearth.

It seemed to Clee that it took him an hour to reach the cabin's doubtful sanctuary. Actually it was but a few minutes. Without knocking, he opened the door, then said softly: "Sam, it's

Clee. I've been shot. I've got to come in."

He entered, shivering violently and terribly weak. He closed the door carefully behind him. Only the strength of his will kept him erect, swaying, clinging to the door frame for support.

He was a ghastly sight. On his left side, blood, diluted by rain, had crimsoned almost the entire length of his body. His right leg, from the calf down, was equally stained. He peered into the gloom of the cabin, made out the suddenly stirring figure of Nanette as she rose to a sitting position on the bed.

Fright was paramount to her expression. "What do you want? You had better go. Sam will kill you."

Clee made a wry grin. "He won't have to, if I step out of that door." He felt savage impatience. "Damn it, a woman is the farthest thing from my thoughts now. I've been shot."

Instantly she swung her legs out of bed, long, palely gleaming legs, bare halfway up her thighs.

Clee leaned back against the door, grinning weakly. He murmured: "I've never seen your legs before. They're as beautiful as the rest of you." He felt himself begin to slip down the door, tried to stop, and found that he could not.

Nanette, with an impatiently angry exclamation, stood up, letting her long nightdress drop to cover her naked legs. Clee's grin froze on his face. The room whirled before him, and suddenly Nanette's arms were supporting him. She was warm and fragrant, yet there was the strength of determination in her arms. She supported him, her body right against him and cried: "Clee! Try hard! Help me get you to the bed!"

He nodded, took a slow and tottering step. His wounded leg buckled beneath him. He released Nanette, so that he would fall alone, but she clung to him and fell with him.

He was conscious of the heat of her nearly naked body beneath the nightdress, the life-giving heat. Her long hair cascaded over his head and face. With the last of his strength, he put his arms about her and locked them tightly.

When Clee awoke, he was warm. He lay in Nanette's bed, with the covers drawn to his chin. Immediately aware of how soiled and bloody his clothes had been, hating the thought of ruining her bed, he moved a hand under the blanket. He had not ruined her bed. His clothes were gone.

The grin began on his pale face, twisting wryly. Light, the gloomy gray of dawn, made a square of dim illumination at the cabin's single window directly before him. This faint light, coupled with the glow of coals on the hearth, illumined the figure which sat so silently beside him, the girl who dozed in the chair beside his bed, a rifle across her knees.

Clee turned carefully, at once racked by the pain in his calf, the sharper pain in his shoulder, and studied her for a long while with eyes that were somber and still. His steady gaze awakened her, and she stirred, opened her eyes, and stared uncomprehendingly at him.

He managed a faint grin and saw her understanding of his presence come. He asked: "How the hell did you do it? How did you get me in here?"

"I'm stronger than I look." Her glance was steady, her eyes large and unreadable, defenseless with her sudden awakening. He flushed unwillingly, for he was thinking of last night, picturing the nightgown-clad girl, struggling, straining to get him out of his clothes, to get his wounds dressed, to get his naked body raised to the bed and covered by blankets. Thinking this way, he saw the mocking humor as it touched her eyes. His sudden laugh was weak, but it was a laugh. "All right. So you got even with me. Where's my clothes?"

Her words were barely audible. "I had to cut them off of you. You won't need them for a while." She colored abruptly and lowered her glance from his. Then she said briskly: "Sam will be back this morning."

"Where's he been?"

"He took the troop out east for some night maneuvering."

"Anybody show up around here last night?"

"No." She hesitated for just an instant, finally asking: "Was it that man, Jeffords, who shot you?"

Clee frowned. "No, I don't think so. Although he was probably behind it." He stirred again, grimaced, and then asked: "How bad am I hurt? Any bones broken?"

"No. A bullet went through the calf of your leg. Another tore up the muscles of your shoulder. You lost a lot of blood. That's why you're so weak."

She stood up and moved across the room. She got the water bucket and started out the door, bucket in one hand, rifle in the other. Clee said: "Leave the rifle. You are in no danger."

Nanette hesitated. Putting weight on his right arm, Clee raised himself to a sitting position. Dizziness was almost overwhelming. "Let me keep the rifle." There was steel in his voice, for he had a sudden remembrance of the voice of the assassin. He had acquired respect for the man's proficiency. The man would not risk recognition by coming to the cabin after Clee while the girl was present. Yet as soon as she left it . . . ?

Nanette frowned. "Perhaps I should stay."

"No. He will probably not come. But if he should, I would hate to have him find me help-less." Clee felt it hard to convince himself that the continuing tracks of the riderless horse would have long confused the ambusher. This was daylight, a good seven or eight hours after the attack. The horse would have been found by now, backtracked, and the Massey cabin located as the only logical refuge which Clee could have found. Even now, the attackers might be waiting in the brushy fringe of timber.

Nanette brought the rifle to him. Clee checked

its charge automatically, examined the percussion cap, and lowered the hammer to half-cock. With the rifle lying negligently beside him, he watched Nanette go, smiling her doubtful, concerned half smile, but as soon as she had gone, he carefully eased himself around until he had the rifle muzzle pointing directly at the door's center with his finger curled comfortably about its trigger.

He heard the dim bang of the bucket Nanette carried as it struck the trunk of a tree. A moment later he heard her clear voice singing. With her gone, he found himself unconsciously comparing her with Sibyl. Sibyl was intoxication, was fire that could consume a man, sear him, sear his mind with the need for her. Sibyl was a rare and deadly drug, having the power to enslave. Sibyl was all of this, and no man could fail to want her.

Clee himself wanted her as he had wanted nothing before in his life. He wanted her, and he knew she was his for the taking. His blood began to heat, thinking of Sibyl, thinking of her eyes last night, wide and pleading and unashamed. He wanted to see good in Sibyl, wanted to believe her story that Jeffords meant nothing to her, for that would make the conquest of her easy. Yet he could not believe it. He could only seem to remember Darrel, limp and dead on wet, green grass. He could only picture Eames Jeffords, tightly holding Sibyl's straining, writhing body against him. Reason told Clee that Sibyl was Jeffords's woman, reason that made lies of her protestations to the contrary.

Suddenly, one awful question blotted all else from Clee's tortured thoughts. Had Jeffords baited his trap last night with Sibyl? Had the trap been set with Sibyl's knowledge and consent? Cold seeped through the heavy blankets into Clee's body as a slight noise outside the cabin brought him suddenly alert. The scuff of a boot? The rasp of cloth against the cabin wall? For a long while he listened, utterly motionless, but finally he relaxed, convinced that the sound was imagined, or the product of the sun's heat against the cabin's eastern wall.

He thought of Nanette Massey. She was as different from Sibyl as night is from day, but Clee admitted that she had power to stir him nearly equaling that of Sibyl. Nanette was like a thousand fathoms of clear, cool water, into which a man could sink — sink until, reaching bottom at last, fire flowed in his veins, burning, reaching his brain as a great burst of flame. Nanette was this, and more. She could be a mocking, humorous companion, a compassionate friend. She was a woman with strength to do what needed doing. She was. . . .

Alternately heated and chilled by his thoughts, Clee now grinned wryly to himself. Again the lightest noise stirred outside beside the door. This time there was no mistaking it. Clee stiffened.

The door flung open with a screech of stiff hinge leather. A short, squat man with sideburns and a long mustache stood in the doorway, un-speaking and unsmiling. His eyes were a pale, ice-green, his mouth a long, thin slash in a dark-tanned face. His was the passionless face of an executioner. Wordlessly he leveled the long-barreled Colt at the bed, thumbed back the hammer.

Clee's rifle kicked violently against him, held as it was with no bracing against his shoulder. Al-most simultaneously, Rogoff's gun roared. A scream lifted from the direction of the creek, a bucket rang against the ground, and Nanette's light footsteps could be heard, pounding toward the cabin in the ensuing, deathly silence.

Nanette burst through the door, leaped heed-lessly across the still body of Rogoff, and plunged to the bedside. Clee lay still as death, the smoking rifle beside him. Acrid powder fumes whirled in the room. With a sharp cry, Nanette flung the blankets back, and her eyes ran the length of his body like a frantic caress. No new blood stained the bed. No new marks marred the muscular perfection of his body. Nanette began to cry silently, her tears over-flowing her eyes and running wetly across her cheeks. Clee groaned and stirred.

Hastily Nanette covered him. Weak from loss of blood, his heart strained by such savage, sudden excitement, Clee had simply fainted. Nanette turned, snatching up the rifle as she did, and advanced upon the still form of Rogoff. Her beautiful, usually serene features were now a study of female savagery. She poked the inert body with the rifle muzzle, and then she saw the stain that had spread from a neat hole in the man's chest.

Clee's voice lifted behind her, a thin voice with no strength: "Get his revolver off the floor and bring it to me. The rifle is no good now. Then get out of the doorway. The others may be coming in."

Nan pried the squat man's revolver from his dead fingers, withdrew another from the exposed waistband of his trousers. Clee chuckled thinly: "That one's mine. Good of him to return it."

He noted the pallor in Nan's face, the increasing tremble that stirred her lower lip. She brought him the guns, fighting for her fleeing control. The door gaped open, and Clee knew she could not shut it without first dragging the body of Rogoff either in or out of it. He would not ask this of her, so he said, making his voice purposely harsh: "Get over by the stove and sit down."

He had seen Nanette's expression as she had turned from the body of Rogoff, had seen its elemental savagery. He knew that this weakness was but a reaction in her, the reaction because she thought the danger was past. He could not help a mental comparison between Nanette's reaction to the threat that Rogoff offered, and what he suspected would have been Sibyl McAllister's reaction. Yet he knew he was being unfair to

Sibyl, by thus comparing her to Nanette, an entirely different type of woman.

Nanette ran to the bedside and snatched one of the heavy revolvers. A scuffing step sounded near the door outside, and she sprang across the room to half crouch beside the stove. Ten feet from the door a man stepped into Clee's vision, peering into the cabin, and Clee snapped a swift shot at him, and afterward was rewarded by a high yell and the sound of running feet.

A voice called: "The hell with Rogoff! He's dead, but that guy in there ain't!"

Immediately, thereafter, a horse snorted, brush crackled, and a flurry of hoofbeats drummed from the clearing, fading quickly with distance.

Clee murmured: "I think they'll let me alone now. I'm sorry to have brought you all this trouble."

For an instant he thought Nanette was going to cry. Her eyes were large, blue as a winter sky, and they held an expression that was wholly unfathomable to Clee. Then her mouth turned soft and full, with the vaguest suggestion of a smile lurking at its corners. She advanced across the room. Her words, surprisingly, contained no reference to their recent danger.

She said softly: "That woman . . . the one at the hotel. Is she the reason you hate Jeffords?"

"Not altogether. She was part of it."

"But you love her." Half a question, half a statement. A plea for denial.

Clee frowned. His answer was wholly honest. "I don't know. I'm damned, if I do. She's like. . . ." He was struck at once with the incongruity and impropriety of discussing one woman with another.

Softness fled from Nanette's face, and for an instant her eyes were stricken. Then this, too, was gone, and there remained only a strong woman's determination. She turned away from the bed so that he might not see the things her expressions revealed so clearly. She was thinking: *I will make you forget her. I will make you forget that you ever knew her. I will have you to myself for several weeks. By the time you are well enough to want me, you will want me, Clee. I'll see to that.*

She turned back to him, serene and smiling and fully confident, thinking: *Sam will be gone other nights. I'll see to that, too.*

Chapter Eight

In mid-morning, Sam Massey returned to the cabin, resplendent in his new uniform of Union blue, decorated with gold braid and captain's bars, gleaming cavalry boots and spurs, wide-brimmed, black cavalry hat. His beard was trimmed neatly. Upon entering the clearing, he bawled: "Nan! Dammit, Nan, come look at me."

Nan waved him in, smiling at his boyish pride.

He grunted — "What the hell?" — at sight of Rogoff's body. He loomed in the doorway, staring at Clee. "What happened?"

Clee told him. A twinkle appeared in Sam's eyes at the sight of Clee's muddy clothes piled in the corner. He stared at Nan until the flush of embarrassment began to pile up in her face. Finally he whistled with mock relief. He said: "You had me scared. I knew Nan was after a man, and for a minute there I thought she'd had to shoot you to get you."

Nan flushed painfully, and her eyes darkened with anger. Sam Massey roared his laughter. Clee himself could not help grinning, but he was feeling anger, too, anger at the embarrassment Sam was causing Nan.

Sam would not let it drop. He said: "You spent the night here with her. I ought to call you out. But I'll let it go, if you'll marry her."

Nan scolded, crimson: "Sam! Stop it!"

Clee said: "Yeah. Cut it out. I'd be a dead man, if it weren't for Nan. If you don't shut up, I'll roll out of here and shut you up."

Sam apparently saw that he had gone far enough. He asked: "Why'd someone want to kill you?"

Clee nodded his head toward the door. "Take a look at him. Maybe you can tell me. I never saw him before in my life."

Sam Massey strode at once to the door, out into the bright, steaming sunlight. Nanette followed, and Clee could hear the murmur of her voice, reproving, insistent. He heard Sam Massey's low whistle, and then the big man was back inside the cabin.

Sam said: "Nick Rogoff. He's a Georgian, and a damned bad one to tangle with. Did your friend Jeffords put him on you?"

Clee shrugged. "It's possible. I never knew Eames to hire his killing done before, though."

"Personal quarrel?"

Clee nodded and saw Nanette frown.

"Rogoff and Jeffords are both Secesh. You sure there ain't more to it than your personal troubles?"

Again Clee shrugged. He murmured thoughtfully: "I offered Eames a fight the night I arrived in Denver. He turned it down."

"I don't like to be nosy. But I might be able to help you figure it out, if I knew what it was all about."

Nan spoke hastily. "I forgot the water. I'll need some for dinner." She moved out of the door, frightened, embarrassed, obviously not wanting to hear the story of Clee's attachment to Sibyl McAllister.

Sam grunted: "What the hell's the matter with her?"

Clee ignored his question. "Jeffords killed a cousin of mine in a duel. I took it up, and he put me in the hospital."

"Fightin' over a woman?"

Clee nodded. "Sibyl McAllister. She's here in Denver now."

"Jeffords's woman?"

Clee's face twisted. "I don't know. Damn it, I don't know. She says she isn't. She seems to hate him."

"You still want her, is that it?"

"I guess it is. What man wouldn't want her? You ever seen her?"

Massey nodded. His massive features were thoughtful. "I didn't know she was acquainted with Jeffords. I've never seen her with him." He frowned. "That's odd in itself, when you get to thinkin' about it. Jeffords is a ladies' man, a chaser. And she's a damned beautiful woman. It ain't natural for him to ignore her like he does." He mused: "I've seen her out with Vic Levy some. Come to think of it, that's about the only one she does see."

"Is Levy a young man?" Jealousy churned in Clee.

Massey laughed. "Hell, no. He's a little squirt. Fifty, mebbe. Gray hair and damned little of it. Fat. Talk is that he wants to marry her."

Sickness was born in Cletus Fahr. He asked quietly: "Is Levy's line the only stageline out of Denver?"

"Uhn-huh." Sam Massey stared for a moment, slowly comprehending. "I see what you're getting at. No one has connected her with Jeffords. He never speaks to her, 'cept for a nod now and then."

Clee was silent, his thoughts painful and disillusioned. He was beginning to see it. Jeffords was charged by the Confederacy with buying guns and equipping a small force. Sibyl, with the same loyalty to the South, was seeing Levy for the sole purpose of extracting from him information as to stage movements and gold shipments. When Sibyl had the information and when Jeffords had the men, then the plan to supply General Sibley in Texas with gold would be put into operation.

If his surmise were true, it was also inevitable that Sibyl was Jeffords's woman. No conceivable coincidence could have put them together in this by chance. Sibyl was Jeffords's mistress. The thought stirred burning rage in Clee's mind. It stirred another thought as well, one that was equally unpleasant. He was the only one in Denver City who could connect Jeffords and Sibyl. It explained the murder attempt.

Depression became a weight in his thoughts. Sibyl must have known about the plan to murder him. She would have taken him into her bed, though, and afterward would have sent him out to his death. But he shook his head savagely, angrily, suddenly ashamed of his own willingness to condemn. He said, perhaps too emphatically: "Sibyl had nothing to do with Rogoff. I took her to dinner last night, and I'm damned if I think she could have hidden it, if she had known I was about to be killed."

Sibyl might be Jeffords's mistress. She might also be with him in the Confederate plot. But she would not join him in plotting Clee's murder.

Sam Massey growled: "I think I'd better have a talk with Levy."

Clee said: "Don't do it. You'll just tip our hand. Sibyl is not an ordinary woman. Levy would never believe you."

Massey scowled. "If we can't trust Levy, then how the hell are we going to know when they're going to strike?"

"Watch Jeffords. Watch the other Rebel hotheads. When they start to gather, then it's time to watch out. They're not all in Denver, Sam. They're up at the mines. Put a few of your boys up there. They ought to be able to tell at least a day before anything happens."

"All right."

Nanette came in timidly, carrying a full bucket of water. She placed it beside the stove. Clee wondered briefly how much of their talk she had heard.

Sam said, grinning slyly again: "I'll leave you

two alone. But behave yourselves."

"Sam!" Nanette stamped a small foot.

Grinning still, Sam went out the door. Clee heard him grunt mightily as he heaved the inert and stiffening body of Rogoff to his saddle. Then, whistling, Sam led the animal past the door and away in the direction of Denver City.

Sibyl McAllister had waited almost the night through for Clee, fully expecting him to return to her. Yet, as the night had worn itself away, she had finally become convinced that he was not coming. At first, this realization stirred the most savage kind of anger in her. She blew out the single lamp she had kept burning and flung herself onto the bed.

She had built within herself a fever of expectancy, a slow-burning bed of coals that waited only for the fuel that Clee himself could add. Now there was nothing left but cold and bitter ashes. Frustration, anger.

"Damn him!" she sobbed. "He's chasing some doxie over on McGaa Street right now." The mental image of Clee satisfying with another woman the passion Sibyl had aroused had the power to turn her white with rage. Her hands fisted and beat at the pillow. She wept, great, tearing sobs that shook the bed upon which she lay. At last, she slept, never knowing that the shots in the street before the hotel earlier this evening, the shots she had so quickly dismissed as some rowdy's private celebration, had been

aimed at Clee and had kept him from a rendezvous that he otherwise might have kept.

All of the next day, Sibyl haunted the Fremont
House lobby. But Clee did not appear. Near sup-
pertime, unable to control herself longer, she approached the desk, smiling warmly at the
bespectacled clerk.

"Has Mister Fahr been in today?"

"No, ma'am." The clerk blushed, his eyes admiring the full curve of Sibyl's breasts. "I haven't
seen him."

"Did you see him last night?"

"Not after he went out with you. Is something
wrong, Miss McAllister?"

"No. Nothing." She turned away and climbed
the stairs toward her room, trying desperately to
hold back the tears of frustration that welled up
unbidden behind her eyes. Her aunt would be
gone for another night, but, after that, a meeting
with Clee might not be so easy. She turned the
handle of her door and opened it, stopping immediately as the wild hope tore through her
breast. Cigar smoke. Clee!

She burst into the room, smiling, hoping.
Then she saw Jeffords.

Jeffords said dryly: "Expecting someone else,
weren't you? Do I disappoint you?"

"Oh, get out! Get out of here! I don't want to
talk to you."

Jeffords's tone was cold. "But I want to talk to
you. What headway are you making with Levy?

93

You've been ignoring him since that damned Fahr arrived."

Sibyl shrugged, then spoke wearily. "I know that the mines are not producing as they should. The men that would ordinarily be working them have quit to join the governor's Volunteers."

"But when is Levy going to ship out the gold?" He rose to his feet and stood facing her, tall, dark-skinned, cynical. Sibyl felt the old, over-powering weakness at his nearness. She wanted to move away, to put the room's breadth between them, but found that she could not. She said wearily: "When he gets enough. It's hard to get information out of that one, Eames. Every time I try to talk anything but trivialities with him, he laughs at me. Tells me such weighty subjects are not for pretty heads like mine."

Jeffords laughed, and even this unpleasant sound had the power to stir Sibyl. "Has he asked you to marry him?"

"Yes."

"What'd you tell him?"

"I put him off."

Eames Jeffords scowled. Sibyl began to tremble, ever so slightly, waiting, waiting until this conversation should be over, until the hunger should show itself in Jeffords's pale eyes, in his cruel and full-lipped mouth. He muttered: "It can't be too long. I know he's got at least a hundred and fifty thousand in his safe. I know he'll want to ship it out before bad weather sets in."

"What do you want me to do?" This was as it had always been. Without trying, simply by being near to her, Jeffords could make her want him, could make her want him so that nothing else was important — not even Clee.

"Tell him you'll marry him. But tell him you have to make a trip East first. Tell him you're afraid to make the trip on the same stage with the gold."

"How will that help?" Ordinarily the question would have been unnecessary. But now, Sibyl's quick mind was dulled with desire.

Jeffords grew suspicious. "When you tell him that, he'll undoubtedly give you some idea of how long you have before any gold will be shipped. A week, two . . . what does it matter? He will be anxious to get you off, so that you'll return sooner. There are only two stages East every week. You begin to put the trip off. Your aunt isn't ready, or you are not quite ready yourself. You will think that you can make each stage, and at the last moment will find that you cannot. Eventually, you will plan on a certain stage and Levy will tell you to let that one go."

"All right, Eames."

A gleam of anticipation danced in his eyes. "We'll be back here in the spring, Sibyl. And we'll fly the Confederate flag over Denver. Then we'll march West . . . to San Francisco . . . to an open seaport on the Pacific. The supplies the South needs will come by sea from Europe, will put into our harbor in San Francisco, unhampered by a Union blockade."

He surprised her now, as he so often did. She thought of him as cruel, self-seeking, lusting after power as he lusted after each new woman who took his fancy. Yet he had this surprising and sincere zeal for the Southern cause. Perhaps his zeal was like all the rest of him, motivated by personal greed, spurred by the knowledge that, when the South came into power, his reward would be great.

Sibyl said softly: "Eames."

"What?"

She moved close, letting her body brush lightly against him. "Eames. Oh, damn you, can't you see? Or don't you want to?"

He laughed, but her anger had struck a spark somewhere within himself. Without touching her, he lowered his mouth, let it touch lightly on her eyes, her parted, eager lips.

Sibyl's thighs ached with the effort of controlling them. Imperceptibly her body arched, until the tips of her breasts brushed against his chest, hotly, frantically eager. Like a lance of fire, her pink tongue darted out, searing his lips, seeking, searching.

For what seemed an eternity, he stood stiffly frozen, letting the fires mount in him, letting Sibyl's own flame rise within her until the need for him became pain, a blinding, torturing, pitiless pain. A moan broke from her lips, and then he seized her, brutally, savagely, ravenously.

She broke away, ran across the room, and blew

out the lamp. In darkness, she stripped the clothes from herself, letting them drop to the floor at her feet. She returned to him, and her hands went inside his shirt, lightly caressing. Her hips writhed, as though from pain. She felt his own strong hands upon her naked body, and then she flung herself backward onto the bed's silken coverlet. Her breasts were white, proud peaks of rose-tipped flesh. Her long, smooth thighs beckoned frantically in the soft glow from the window.

Jeffords was panting, cruel, hungry as he flung his hard-muscled weight upon her. The bed of coals that burned white hot in the core of her being now sent up long, scalding streams of flame as he piled fuel upon them. There was intolerable ecstasy in this endless moment.

There was no tenderness in Jeffords, only this brutal, compelling savagery that was in itself so very satisfying. Sibyl's exhaustion held her motionless on the bed long after he had gone, completely rested and at peace.

Chapter Nine

Vic Levy was not a tall man. He came, in fact, only to Sibyl McAllister's shoulder, when he stood beside her. He was not tall, but neither was he a fool. He was under no illusions as to why Sibyl had consented to marry him. Sibyl was a woman used to luxury. Since Vic Levy operated the stageline, he was in a position to know that Ralph McAllister's claim had not been paying off as had been hoped. Therefore, he reasoned, Sibyl was interested in marriage to himself only for the material things he could provide for her.

He did not resent this. He was grateful to her, pleased to be getting her under any terms. He was also aware that he could not give her all of the things a beautiful woman would want. But he could give her a part of them. And the others . . . ? Vic frowned whenever he thought of it, for he knew she would find the things he could not give her elsewhere. It was the one barb that marred his utter content.

Still, by the time a man reached Vic's age, he had learned to take the bad with the good. So he quieted the doubt within himself, but he wished she would stop vacillating and leave on her trip for the East. He was becoming impatient.

Early in October, he picked her up one afternoon at the Fremont House and drove her out along the river road. Sibyl was dressed warmly in a woolen dress and coat, dressed against the chill, October wind. Yet even heavy clothing could not diminish her charm. She had an aura of fragrance about her, warm humor in her eyes, a smile on her full, red lips.

Levy said: "There is a stage on Wednesday. Will you be able to make it?" His voice was hopeful, almost pleading. He went on: "I am getting anxious, my dear. I am not a young man, but I can still be impatient. Besides, traveling is going to get worse as the winter comes on. I should not like to think you were any more uncomfortable than was necessary."

Sibyl's regret seemed genuine enough. Indeed, it was. Although Levy could not know it, Sibyl was beginning to feel ashamed. She regretted the use to which Levy was being put. She had honestly begun to like the little man, to respect his gentleness and his consideration.

The buggy whirled along the dusty road, down magic corridors of bright, golden cottonwood leaves. Ducks rose from the river as they passed, mallards with their bright green heads — teal, each with a brilliant spot of blue-gray on its wings. A wedge of geese drove past overhead, honking dismally.

Levy drew her arm through his.

Sibyl said: "I'm sorry, Vic. It's Aunt. She keeps putting it off. Perhaps next week."

"Well, be sure you make it then. The gold is going out the first of the following week, and I don't know why you should be afraid to ride on the stage that carries it. We have not had a robbery in over six months." He smiled at her. "But I respect your wishes, my dear."

Sibyl could not help the elation that surged through her. Neither could she help the shame that colored her face. Her voice was subdued. "All right, Vic. We'll go next week."

He leaned over and kissed her cheek, warmly exuberant. "Good! That's a promise, then."

He clucked to the buggy horse, slapped its back with the reins. His face was beaming. Sibyl smiled at him, but she could not keep her thoughts on him. She kept thinking of Clee. Nearly a month had passed since he had been shot. Sibyl had not seen him because Jeffords claimed that to do so might jeopardize her position with Levy. But she had questioned Sam Massey as to the extent of his injuries, had discovered that while they could have been serious, while they were still painful, they were healing satisfactorily under Nanette's care.

Rogoff had been buried with little ceremony the day Massey had brought his body into town. Sibyl had broken finally and decisively with Jeffords the following day, when she learned of the attack. Now she thought: *Next week I'll go East on the stage. And I won't be coming back.*

She realized suddenly that, since she had the information she wanted from Levy, she could see Clee. *But what good will that do?* she asked herself bitterly.

100

Levy looked at her questioningly and murmured: "You're very thoughtful today, my dear. You are not regretting our bargain?"

She squeezed his arm. "Of course not, Vic." She felt a stir of pity. Bargain, indeed! He had made a bargain. But Sibyl had not. She would be gone by the time he realized it.

All of the way back to town, she sat very close to him, her arm linked in his. She was thinking: *I'll be good to him until I go. I'll see him all I can in the time that's left. Maybe that will help him, when he realizes what I have done.*

She kept thinking of Clee, alone with Massey's sister in the one-room cabin. She had seen Nanette several times in town, had each time felt an overpowering jealousy, an outright dislike for the girl. She knew she was being unfair and purely woman-like in this, but she could not help herself.

Sibyl's own life was a mess, largely because of Eames Jeffords. If he had never come to the Fahr plantation, if he had not been attracted to her, if he had not taken her in his arms . . . if! Sibyl would have married Darrel, could have been happy with him. Even after Darrel's death, if Jeffords had let her alone, if he had not followed her, she might still have returned, might still have had Clee.

Now, Sibyl was beginning to realize, it was too late. She tried to tell herself that even here in Denver she might have salvaged something. Clee was no longer a romantic boy. He was a man,

101

with a man's sharp hungers. Perhaps if Sibyl could have coaxed him to her room the night he'd been shot . . . ? Perhaps if he could have known the intensity of her love, the violence of her passion for him, things might even then have been different. But he had not come to her room, had instead been shot, and at Jeffords's direction. Wounded, he had gone to Massey's. And he had been thrown into daily and continuous contact with the beautiful Nanette Massey. Sibyl was under no illusions about Nanette. Clee was a man that any woman would want. Nanette would want him, too.

Levy was watching her, an odd, worried look on his face. Sibyl composed her expression with difficulty. The buggy whirled into town and, after a few moments, drew up before the Fremont House. Vic jumped to the ground, balding and fat, his gallantry almost ridiculous. Sibyl kissed him lightly and fled into the hotel.

She had done her job. She had done it well. She had obtained information for Jeffords that he could not have obtained otherwise, and now she was free. Yet there was no satisfaction in that, no feeling at all other than relief. She had helped the Confederacy, but she had not been able to help herself.

She stopped at the desk, scribbled a note to Jeffords. She climbed the stairs and, as she went past his room, hastily glanced up and down the hall, then stooped and slipped the note under his door. She went on up to her own room.

Hardly had she finished removing her coat when Jeffords knocked and burst into the room. He was excited, very plainly so. Sibyl looked at him with outright dislike. She said: "This is a cruel thing to do to Vic Levy."

He looked at her sardonically. "A poor time to start worrying about that. What did you find out?"

"The gold will go out week after next. The first stage."

"Good." His eyes glowed. "Now we can get moving. I've got all the guns I need, and I've got my men picked. Forty of them. We don't need that many, but Sibley can use them."

"I am leaving next week," Sibyl said. "I'm not coming back."

He came toward her. "You'll come back. By the first of May. Denver will be ours."

Sibyl shook her head coldly.

Jeffords asked, frowning: "You're holding out for marriage this time, aren't you?"

He was so sure of her — so confident. Few women had ever been able to stand against him. Yet Sibyl was seeing him in a new light today. He was vain, egotistical. He was supremely selfish. He was cruel. He could arouse Sibyl, could satisfy the passion he aroused, but he could never make her happy. He could never make any woman happy. He was a man who took, but who never returned anything to replace that which he took.

She said: "Eames, I used to hate you. But I'm

just beginning to see that there isn't enough of you to hate. I'm going East next week, and I'm not coming back. I don't want to see you again." She went to the door and held it open. "Good bye, Eames. I've given you the information you want." Her voice became brittle. "Perhaps getting the information was right. But the method I used to get it was not."

He laughed, kissing her lightly as he passed. He did not believe her. He was too sure of himself to believe her now. But after she had gone . . . ?

Strangely, the touch of his lips had not stirred her. She thought wildly as she closed the door: *I've won! I am really finished with him this time.* But she felt no real elation, felt only an unconquerable depression. Listless, she began to pack.

At first dark, a wagon pulled away from the Elephant Corral, drawn by two teams, and made its way uptown. It pulled into an alley just below McGaa and drew up behind a long, log warehouse. Soames climbed down from the seat. A figure came from the shadows, and the warehouse door creaked open. Soames spread a canvas in the wagon bed, and the two began to load.

They worked silently, swiftly. When the guns and ammunition were all loaded, Soames spread a second canvas over them. He added a layer of inch boards. Then he and Jeffords began to load provisions on top of the boards. When the wagon was full, still another canvas went over the top.

Jeffords was sweating.

Soames said: "I'll travel all night. By this time tomorrow night, I'll be there."

Jeffords nodded. "I'll follow you, horseback, tomorrow."

He watched the heavily laden wagon as it creaked to the end of the alley. Then he swung the warehouse door shut and snapped the padlock on it. A pair of drunken troopers on a foraging expedition entered the alley, and Jeffords stepped back into the shadows. He grinned to himself at their lack of interest in the wagon. They came past Jeffords, unsuspecting of his presence. He thought: *There goes a load of Confederate guns, boys, and you don't even know it.*

Each of them carried a burlap sack. Jeffords watched them curiously. The wagon had turned into the street and now was out of sight. Halfway down the alley, the two stopped. They melted into the shadows beside a small outbuilding, and a few seconds later Jeffords heard the aroused squawk of chickens.

He began to smile. Someone burst from the back door of the house, running. The two troopers, each carrying a squirming sack, ran past him.

A voice bawled: "Stop, dammit, or I'll blow the pants offen ya!"

Jeffords thought, too late. *I'd better get out of here.* He began to run, perhaps twenty feet behind the troopers. As he ran, he cursed the troopers, cursed his own impulsive foolishness.

He should have stayed where he was, yet he could realize that staying might have been exceedingly dangerous. It was obvious that the irate chicken owner carried some kind of gun. If he had discovered Jeffords, hiding beside the warehouse, the range would have been point-blank, and Jeffords would have been forced to kill him in self-defense.

Jeffords felt the sharp pain of buckshot the briefest instant before he heard the roar of the scatter-gun. He stumbled, fell. The troopers scurried out of the alley, turned the corner, and disappeared. Jeffords could hear pounding feet in the alley, his pursuer's triumphant yell: "Got one, by God! Now maybe them damned troops will leave my chickens alone."

The man was but twenty yards away. He slowed, slowed to a walk, and approached Jeffords cautiously. Jeffords did not try to get his feet under him, for he could not know how badly he was hurt. He could feel the burn of shot in half a dozen places. He eased the long Colt from its holster. Still the man approached. He said, nervousness and fear showing now in his voice: "Sing out, buster. Sing out, or I'll let you have it again."

Jeffords raised his gun. The man's body was a dark blur before him. He aimed by instinct, for there was no seeing the gun's sight in this light.

Suddenly, the man saw his gun. He started to dive aside, but he was too late. Jeffords's ball took him in the abdomen, and he buckled, stood hunched in the alley for a moment, then crumpled to the ground.

Jeffords pushed himself to his knees. His buttocks and the backs of his thighs were soaked with blood. But he could walk. He got to his feet. He hurried away.

Flesh wounds. But they could not have come at a more inopportune time. During the next week he had a lot of riding to do, a lot of extremely important riding. He was needed to organize the stage robbery, the flight from it later. Furthermore, there was likely to be repercussions from this killing tonight. It would be blamed on the troops, undoubtedly upon Captain Massey's foraging company. Yet, if Jeffords called in a doctor to remove the buckshot . . . ?

He scowled blackly, bitter anger rising in him. He had planned this so damned carefully. He had been aware that the sudden departure from the mines of forty Southern sympathizers would not go unnoticed. He had planned to take the stage with no more than half a dozen men, including himself. He had intended that Soames should leave the mines with the balance of the men before dawn the day of the robbery and meet him, by swift travel, some forty or fifty miles south of Denver City, from there on to form a rear guard for the looted stage.

Now, unless he were able to ride to the mines, Soames would have complete charge of the thing. And Soames would probably bring the whole forty men to Denver, where their sudden appearance could not help being noticed.

Jeffords thought: *Buckshot or not, I've got to ride tomorrow.* He considered the few lukewarm Southern sympathizers he knew within the confines of Denver, rejected them one by one. There weren't any he could trust implicitly.

His face flamed with futile rage as he fought the only logical solution to his predicament. Sibyl. Damn her, how she'd laugh. But there was no help for it. No help at all. If he tried to ride with the shot in him, his wounds would fester and swell and grow sorer until he could no longer sit a saddle.

Determinedly refusing to limp, his face contorted with rage and pain, he strode into the Fremont House lobby. He was thankful for the full cloak that partially concealed his legs. Mounting the stairs was torture.

He hesitated before his own door, finally went inside. Perhaps with a mirror. . . . He took the mirror from the wall and propped it against a table. He took off his cloak, and dropped his trousers. He took a knife from his pocket, held the blade in lamplight until it was hot. Then he went after a round shot embedded perhaps half an inch in the calf of his leg.

He winced and drew back as the hot knife touched raw flesh. He clenched his teeth and tried again. Sweat broke out on his forehead. Nausea stirred in his stomach, and faintness came to his brain. With a sudden, vicious gesture, he flung the knife across the room. He yanked his trousers up. He shrugged into his cloak, and went out, slamming the door behind him.

He was surly when Sibyl came to the door. He pushed her aside and went in. He said: "Damn you, if you laugh at me, I'll kill you! Soames and I loaded the guns, and Soames got away all right with the wagon. But a pair of damned troopers came into the alley to raid a hen house. The landowner had a shotgun, and I got it instead of the troopers."

Sibyl's face was still, yet Jeffords thought he could see the taunting humor hiding behind her bland eyes. He said: "You've got to get it out for me. I've got to ride tomorrow, and I can't ride with this damned shot in me." He thought he detected a new glow in her eyes, one that looked almost like pleasure, like anticipation.

She said meekly: "All right, Eames. Take your trousers off. Lie down on the bed."

Scowling and surly, he did as she told him. She brought a knife. She heated its end in the flame. Jeffords buried his face in the pillow, clutched the bedstead with both hands. He knew suddenly what the glow was that he had seen in her eyes. She wanted to make him pay, now, for the pain he had caused her in the past.

The knife dug deeply into his leg, twisted, twisted again. Sibyl said softly: "Oh Eames, I'm sorry. I didn't get it. I'll have to try again." His body was bathed with sweat. Consciousness was slipping away. With the last of it, just before the knife touched him again, he flung his head around and looked at her.

She was smiling, white-faced, but smiling. She had said she was through with him, but he hadn't believed it. Until now. The knife touched his leg again, and, as it did, Sibyl's eyes met his. A scream started in his throat, and he pushed his face into the pillow. The pain continued, as sharply as before, but immediately, as it stopped, Sibyl sobbed: "I can't do it. I can't. I can't torture you, Eames, no matter how you've hurt me."

She was silent for a long moment. Jeffords could smell the knife heating. When Sibyl spoke again, her voice was small and calm. "I'll get them out now, as quickly as I can."

And Jeffords held on — and waited.

Chapter Ten

Sam Massey dismounted before the cabin and swung to the ground. His bearded face was clouded with worry. Morning sun beat down into the clearing, and a light covering of snow lay upon the ground. Smoke curled up from the chimney, and the smell of frying side meat was in the air. He pushed open the door.

Clee sat at the table, a homemade crutch propped against the wall beside him. Nanette stood before the stove, her face flushed from its heat. She said: "You must have gotten up early, Sam."

"I did." He scowled. "A man was killed in Denver last night. Some thieves raided his chicken house. When he took after them with a shotgun, one of them shot him. They're claiming the thieves were some of my boys. The dead man's wife says they've been raiding the hen house every night, and last night her husband had enough. He told her, when he went out, that he was going to get one of them."

Clee asked: "Was it your boys, Sam?"

"That's what worries me. I think it was. But I can't imagine any of them killing someone over a few chickens. They know I would stand behind them."

He went over to the stove, lifted a long slice of

111

half-cooked bacon from the skillet with his fingers. Chewing on it, he said: "They haven't been paid since I brought them here. I spend half my time trying to get decent rations for them. I don't blame them for foraging, but I won't stand for murder."

He sat down across the table from Clee. Nan poured him coffee. He gulped it, his frown deepening. "I can't stay to investigate it, either. Almost a month ago we sent an escort of thirty men to Fort Laramie. They're not back yet, and we've had no news of them. I've got to take a dozen men and go look for them."

Clee asked: "Can I help you, Sam?"

"No, I guess not. Champion is at the barracks. The other lieutenant, Holbrook, took the escort detail." He began to grin tightly. "I rousted the governor out of bed this morning as soon as I heard. I told him he'd have to do something, or I was going to mount the company and take them East. He said he would."

"What can he do?" Nanette asked.

"He says the government in Washington won't give him any funds, and that there's nothing in the territorial treasury he can use to maintain troops. So he's going to issue some drafts on the U.S. Treasury."

Clee grinned. "Can he do that?"

Sam shrugged. "He says he can."

Clee shook his head. "He'll get in trouble. The government won't stand for it."

"He'll be in a hell of a lot worse trouble, if he

112

don't get some money. I haven't lost any deserters, but the rest of the regiment has. My troop is out of patience, and they're going to start living off the town altogether, if something ain't done. There's talk in Denver of organizing a police force to defend the town from soldiers. If they do that, you know what'll happen. Nothing but fights, nothing but killings."

Clee queried thoughtfully: "How long will you be gone?"

Massey shrugged. "I'll be damned if I know. A week . . . two."

"What if something comes up on this Jeffords business?"

Massey shook his head. "You and Champion will have to handle it. I've got three men up at the mines, watching, claiming they're deserters. If there's any word, they'll get it to you."

Clee thought of Nanette, alone with him in the cabin while Sam would be gone. He said: "I'll go back to the hotel."

Nanette faced him, hands on hips. "You will not! You're not well yet, not by a long sight!"

Clee grinned at her. "What about your reputation?"

She colored furiously. Clee stared at her, and she turned her back on him. Sam looked from one to the other. He was beginning to see something he had not seen before. So that was the way it was with Nanette? He began to grin, but stifled the grin as she turned. Her eyes were pleading. Sam said: "Let me worry about her reputation.

You're in no shape to go back to town yet. Jeffords might have another try at you."

"But . . . ?"

Nanette said maliciously: "He doesn't like it here. He doesn't like my cooking."

"You know that isn't it."

Sam said impatiently: "Then shut up. You're staying."

Clee shrugged.

Nanette shot a glance of gratitude at her brother, but her eyes dropped too quickly away, and the color seeped up again into her face.

What the hell's she up to? wondered Sam. He finished his breakfast and got to his feet. "I've got to get going. Don't look for me till you see me coming."

He stuffed a double handful of biscuits into his pocket. Clee got up and hobbled to the door. Sam looked back once, and then he went out of sight in the trees.

Clee stood at the door, pensively soaking in the morning sunlight. Nanette watched him covertly. The panic that had been in her eyes was subsiding, replaced by an odd, girlish fright. She felt as she had many times when a little girl, planning something she knew would not have the approval of her parents.

Clee had been getting increasingly restless. Essentially a man of action, she supposed the inaction was getting on his nerves, as was his own helplessness and dependence upon her. She

114

watched him more than he knew. There were times, many times, when she was sure his thoughts were on Sibyl McAllister, and at these times she would feel an overwhelming depression. For she admitted to herself that she loved Clee. She also admitted that while he was strongly attracted to her, he still had Sibyl's intoxication in his blood.

Nanette had made it a point to see Sibyl. The first time, she had made a pretense of having lost something at the Fremont House and had waited in the hotel lobby, while the clerk had searched through the hotel's lost articles. She had seen Sibyl several times since, and each time had felt a sense of the hopelessness of having to compete with such a gorgeous creature. That Sibyl's attraction was chiefly physical, Nanette had gradually realized. Therefore, she reasoned, she must fight the woman on the same ground. She had made herself a low-cut nightgown which afterward she had been afraid to wear. But now, watching Clee, so still and thoughtful in the doorway, she resolved: *I'll wear it tonight.*

Immediately she had a guilty feeling that she was fighting with weapons that were not quite fair. Clee hobbled outside and settled himself against the cabin wall in the sun. Nanette began to wash the breakfast dishes, afterward got the broom and swept the floor. She made up both beds, changing Clee's, blushing furiously as she did so.

The inane cliché — *All is fair in love and war.* —

kept running through her mind. She brushed her gleaming black hair much longer than was necessary, braided it, and wound the braids around her head. *Why isn't it fair to fight for him?* she asked herself angrily. *Sibyl will bring him nothing but despair. She has been Eames Jeffords's woman, and she will be someone else's after she gets Clee.*

The morning dragged. Clee sat in the sun and cleaned his guns. During the afternoon, he heated lead on the stove and poured bullets in a mold on the table. Twice, he got up and wandered out of sight into the timber. But at last he lay down on the bed and went to sleep.

Nanette took a towel, a bar of soap, and went down to the creek. There was a place, a sharp bend in the course of the stream, where a deep pool had collected, screened by timber on three sides, sheltered by a bluff on the fourth. All of the light snow had melted from the ground. The sun was warm and bright. Nanette slipped out of her clothes, stood for a moment at the edge of the water, savoring the cool caress of the breeze upon her nakedness.

She looked at her body, thinking of Clee. Her hips were full and round, her abdomen strong-muscled and lightly rounded. Her waist was tiny, her breasts above it full and proud, tipped with hard, firm nipples. She plunged into the icy water, then came out, and soaped herself thoroughly. She plunged back in and rinsed. During early fall, while the days were warm, she had greatly enjoyed this daily plunge. Now, there was

116

little enjoyment in it. The water was too cold, and, once her body was wet, the wind felt like ice upon it.

She dried herself briskly and slipped into her clothes. She went back to the house. Clee stood at the woodpile, chopping wood. She paused before him, her face fresh-scrubbed and shining, her smile warm. Excitement stirred her. She saw that he winced every time he struck a blow with the axe. He was grim and still-faced.

Nanette said: "We don't need any wood."

He scowled at her. Then he stopped, and laid aside the axe. "I know it. I don't know what's the matter with me."

Nanette touched his face with a soft hand, and went on.

Clee had said he did not know what was the matter with him. He admitted now, watching her shapely back as she walked toward the cabin, that he had lied. Everyday it became harder for him to maintain an impersonal friendliness between himself and Nanette. He was healing, getting well, and the old, male hungers were stirring in him.

When he was with Nanette, the face and form of Sibyl were far away, as was the irresistible pull of her against him. Yet when he was alone . . . sometimes in the night . . . those were the times that Sibyl returned to haunt him, to torture him as he thought of her, perhaps even then in Eames Jeffords's arms.

A thousand times he asked himself — *How can*

a man love two women at once? — but he never found the answer. He tried desperately to convince himself that Sibyl was a fantasy in his mind. He tried to convince himself that she was unscrupulous, that she could no more stay true to one man than Eames Jeffords could stay true to one woman. Yet even these things had little effect on her recurring image in his thoughts. And these recurring thoughts of her made him doubt the fire than ran in his veins when Nanette was near to him, when she brushed lightly against him at the table, when she came across the room each night in her nightgown to blow out the lamp before retiring to her own bed behind the curtain that was drawn between them.

Clee acknowledged a great obligation both to Nanette and to Sam. They had taken him in, had saved his life. He would neither betray Sam's trust, nor Nanette's hospitality. Yet he was human. He knew the strength of his desire for Nan. So each day, in late afternoon, he tried to exhaust himself, either by walking, by carrying water, or by chopping wood.

It would have been easy, so very easy, simply to ask Nanette to marry him. He was almost sure she would say yes. A man had a feel for these things. Unless he was a complete fool, he could sense a woman's desire, could tell when her glance was warm and personal. Yes, Nanette would accept him, and the very thought of possessing her, of continuing this wonderful relationship with her forever, had the power to speed his heart, to make the blood throb in his veins. But it wouldn't be fair to Nanette. The ghost of Sibyl, no matter how he tried, would be forever between them.

In sudden anger, he kicked a block of wood halfway across the yard. Then, quieting, he stooped and gathered up the wood he had chopped. His shoulder was nearly healed, yet there was much stiffness in it and, when he moved it, pain. He could walk a little now without the crutch, but it was a painful business, and his limp was pronounced.

Using the crutch, he made his way across the yard. He laid it aside at the door, moved inside, and dumped the wood beside the stove, atop the already large pile.

Nanette said: "You're restless. That's a good sign. You're getting well." She laid a hindquarter of venison on the table and cut off several steaks. She picked up the quarter of meat and returned it to the lean-to where Sam had lately been sleeping.

Clee said: "I'll move out there tonight." He would not look at her.

Nanette came over to him, stood close. The clean fragrance of her rose to his nostrils. Her eyes were so dark they appeared almost purple. She asked — "Why?" — and there was deliberate provocation in her glance. "Are you worrying about my reputation?" She swayed against him, her face lifted, a pale, sweet oval in the fading light that sifted in through the open door.

She seemed to sear, to burn him where she touched. And suddenly his arms were around her, strong and tight. She flung herself hard against him. Her lips were soft, warm.

Her hands, strong, possessive hands, moved up his back, behind his head. Her fingers knotted themselves in his hair. She began to tremble. Clee, with a desperate effort, tore free and thrust her away. He started for the door.

"Where are you going?"

"To saddle a horse," he said harshly, and hobbled on.

Lightly she put herself in the doorway before him. "No."

He looked down at her. "Do you want me to stay here with you after what has happened? You know that will not be all, don't you?"

Her eyes were naked, unashamed. "I know."

"And you want it that way?"

She nodded, her eyes unwavering.

Clee asked brutally: "Do you know what you're getting into? Is this the first time?"

Now, suddenly, she hesitated and seemed unsure.

He asked again: "Is it?"

He had no way of divining the debate that raged within her. If she told him yes, she would be unable to keep him here. If she said no, he might think less of her, it might even cool his ardor and lose her his love forever. Abruptly she seemed to come to some decision. She shook her head, then flung her arms around his neck, and buried her face in his chest.

Her answer was a shock to Clee. He could not deny it. He did not know she was lying, was desperate, would do anything at all to keep him here. Yet she was so sweet against him, so indescribably tender. He tilted her face up. Tears glistened in her eyes, made a path across her cheeks. She said simply: "Please, Clee."

To refuse would have been brutal. And Clee did not want to refuse. He nodded. "All right."

Now, suddenly, she was shy. "I'll get your dinner."

Tension and excitement were plain in her. Clee's feelings were a strange combination of guilt and wild excitement. Nanette fairly flew at her task. Clee, because he could not trust his feelings, went outside. Night had come down, early night when the world is deep gray. He could see only the fringe of trees across the clearing. The creek made its soft murmur against the night's silence. He did not know how long he stood, his body hot, his hands trembling. Clee had known many women, but never had his feelings been like this.

Nanette called him from the doorway — "Supper, darling." — and he went in.

Her cheeks were flushed, her eyes very bright. Her smile was tender, loving. Her own hands trembled as she poured his coffee. Clee thought: *No, I can't do it. I've got to go.* But he was caught in a trap as old as mankind.

Both of them ate with silent concentration.

Once, Clee looked up, found her eyes upon him, peculiarly defenseless, wholly sweet. She smiled.

There was nothing rational in the things she did afterward. She picked up the dishes and washed them as though this night were no different than any other. Clee sat in a chair and watched her, a sort of wonder in his eyes. When she had finished, she drew the curtain between the two beds and retired behind it. He could hear the rustling as she removed her clothes.

He remembered the first night — that night at the way station just outside of Denver City. Then she came out to him. She wore a long, white nightgown. Cut low, it showed him plainly the curve of her breasts, the delicious valley between. She advanced across the room, each step molding the sheer gown against her body beneath. She was shy, but she was not frightened. She went around the end of the curtain and climbed into Clee's bed. Clee blew out the lamp. After a few moments he got in beside her.

Chapter Eleven

Gray dawn was filtering through the cabin window, when Nanette awoke. Her hair lay spread about her on the pillow. Carefully, ever so slightly, she turned her head until she could look at Clee. His face was relaxed. There was the lightest kind of a smile on his mouth. His was a strong face, but this morning Nanette knew she had read it right during the stage journey to Denver. Clee could be hard. There was wildness in him, but there was gentleness, too.

Just the memory of that gentleness put a soft smile on her lips. He was warm beside her, his body hard and thin from his wounds. There was soaring happiness in Nanette's heart. She moved closer, and a hand went up to stroke his cheek.

He opened his eyes.

Nanette murmured: "Good morning, darling." Sleepily he drew her close, but after a moment she pulled away, saying: "Let me get up. It's daylight."

Clee sat on the edge of the bed, and reached for his trousers. Nanette slipped from beneath the covers, crossed the floor, and ducked behind the curtain. She dressed rapidly. But when she came out, Clee was shaking down the ashes in the stove. He built a fire, and Nanette put on the coffee pot.

Oddly, after their complete intimacy of last night, a constraint was growing up between them this morning. Nanette could feel it, and it puzzled her. She got the hindquarter of venison from the place where it hung in the lean-to, and brought it in. Clee went outside to wash, and, when he returned, he took a place at the table, silent and thoughtful. Nanette poured him a cup of coffee.

She thought she knew what was bothering him. Guilt. Remorse, knowing that she had lied to him in saying it would not be the first time for her. A feeling that he had betrayed both Sam Massey and Nanette. Tears glistened suddenly in Nanette's eyes. She did not want it this way. There should be no guilt for something as beautiful as last night.

Why must humans be so complex? Why could they not take life's wonderful gifts with no questions and no doubts?

She waited, for there was nothing else she could do. Whatever problems and doubts had built themselves in Clee's mind could be settled only by Clee himself. She diced some boiled potatoes and fried them with the steak. She made a pan of biscuits. When the food was all on the table, she sat down across from Clee.

He reached a hand across the table, squeezed Nanette's own. His face was unsmiling, very thoughtful. A sudden fear began to build in Nanette. Then he said: "Marry me, Nan."

Nanette could feel the blood draining from her face. Oh, why didn't he smile? Why didn't he come around the table, yank her to her feet, ask her in the way a woman wants to be asked?

Marriage was what Nan wanted. So why didn't she say yes? She wanted Clee. Why, then, did she not take him? As though from a far distance, she saw herself, saw her head shaking. A voice that did not sound like her own parried: "Because of last night? Or because you want me?"

Was it woman's inconsistency that desired ardor to the proposal equal to the ardor he had shown loving her? He had not asked her to marry him before last night. She did not want marriage with him because of it.

That she herself had maneuvered him deliberately into taking her, she had to admit. Fear of Sibyl had led her to that, fear that, when Clee was well, he would go back to Sibyl and forget her. She loved and wanted Clee, or she could not have given herself to him. Yet she did not want his gratitude, nor did she want him because he felt either ashamed or obligated.

Clee was honest with his answer to her question, which in itself was wrong at a time like this. He said thoughtfully: "I guess what happened has something to do with my asking you this morning. I have been thinking of Sam. I have been thinking that I owe you a great deal." Something must have told him that this was the wrong tack, for he said hastily: "Nan, Nan, I love you. I want to marry you because I do."

A kind of cold terror was growing in Nan. She could feel her body trembling. She told herself frantically: *Stop this! Stop it! This is not what you want at all!* Her head was shaking, and her words seemed to come from her mouth through no volition on her part. "No. I won't marry you!" Suddenly she was wildly angry. "You act as though I were a . . . a common woman whose price is marriage! You act as though you were ready to pay it!"

Clee had paled and now looked miserably unsure of himself, terribly puzzled and confused. Almost as though he had asked the words, his expression revealed his thought: *What did I say? What did I do that was wrong?*

Nanette wanted to rush around the table, wanted to fling herself into his arms, to resolve this miserable misunderstanding before it went further, before it built a chasm between them. She heard her own cold voice: "You feel guilty about last night. You're all mixed up. I don't want you that way. I don't want you at all!"

Nan knew suddenly that she was going to cry. She sprang to her feet, evaded his reaching hands, and sped out the door. Clee hobbled after her, trying desperately to run. At the door he stumbled. His bad leg went out from under him, and he sprawled in the dirt.

Nanette was halfway across the clearing. Her tears blinded her; her sobs deafened her to the slight noise he made in falling. She did not see the terrible, anguished expression on his face. She did not see his hopeless rage, for she did not look back.

126

For more than an hour she wandered along the bank of Cherry Creek, in its golden-leafed, frost-bitten bottoms. When she returned to the cabin, Clee was gone.

Frantic, Nanette ran to the corral, nearly hidden in the trees on the bank of the creek. His horse was gone, too. Still-faced and pale, she went into the cabin and sat down. Her anger was gone, her hurt and disappointment. So was her hope. For a long while she stared blankly and emptily at the wall. Then she got up and began to wash the dishes.

In the afternoon, she walked the mile to Denver City. At the Elephant Corral, she hired a surrey and a man to drive it. In the surrey, she returned to the cabin, packed her clothes and her few treasured personal belongings, and had them loaded in the surrey.

Then she climbed up to the seat beside the driver. "Take me to the Planter's House," she said quietly.

She looked back as the surrey bounced off, picking its careful way through the scattered timber. Tears stood out in her eyes. She hated leaving this place where she had been so poignantly happy. But she knew she could never bear the loneliness of the cabin for the weeks that Sam would be gone. She knew she would be unable to bear the torture of memory. Every time she looked at Clee's bed, the misery of being without him would strike her, every time she cooked a meal. In the night-silent darkness of the cabin, she would listen for his even breathing. She would wake and reach her arms out for him.

He was gone, gone from her life forever. Her own face flushed again with shame as she thought of last night. She had given all she had to give him, and it had not been enough. Really, what she had to offer was so little. She knew nothing of love, of men. Sibyl, with her greater experience, could give Clee so much more.

Unutterable depression overcame her. The rig moved into Denver, passed the Fremont House where Clee was undeniably staying again. Nanette kept her glance straight ahead. They turned the corner, and after a few more moments drew up before the imposing bulk of the Planter's House. The driver assisted Nan to the ground, then followed her in, carrying her bags.

Wearily she signed the register and climbed the stairs. Alone in the room at last, she threw herself down across the bed. For a while, she was tense and very still, but at last her tears came, and her bitter sobs. And, eventually, she slept.

Slowly the days dragged past. Wind whipped out of the north day after day, tearing leaves from the cottonwoods in great clouds, raising dust from the streets. It snowed, and it cleared. At the mines on the Vasquez, although each man had his orders, activity went on with its tiresome sameness. Eames Jeffords returned to Denver. On Tuesday, the day before Sibyl was to leave, he came into the Planter's House just as Nanette was moving across the lobby toward the dining room. A smile crossed his frowning face at the sight of her, and he removed his hat.

Nan would have gone on past, but Jeffords caught her arm. "This is a real pleasure," he murmured. "Clee has been monopolizing you, but since he is well, there is no longer any excuse for that. Will you have your dinner with me?"

Nan felt a certain revulsion, for she suspected that Jeffords had been behind the shooting of Clee. He was also a Rebel. Yet she could not escape the man's positive attraction, and she was desperately in need of something to restore her wounded pride, her lost confidence.

She started to shake her head, but Jeffords asked swiftly: "You are not waiting for Clee, are you?" He smiled. "I thought that, if you were, you might have a long wait. He went out in a buggy early this morning with Miss McAllister, and they have not returned yet."

Jealousy stabbed through Nan.

Jeffords pressed his advantage instantly. "There are few beautiful women in this dismal place. You would honor me."

There was so much anxiety upon his face that Nan could not help smiling. She said: "All right."

"Good." He held out his arm, and Nan took it. It was hard and muscular beneath her hand. She was piqued that Clee had so quickly sought solace in Sibyl McAllister, but then she thought: *Solace for what? He is not hurt because he does not have me. I was his nurse and an outlet for his need and nothing else.* Her anger stirred anew.

Yet her jealousy persisted as she thought of Clee and Sibyl side by side in a buggy somewhere on the lonely prairie. This jealousy made her smile at Jeffords particularly warm. Almost unconscious was her desire to hurt Clee by being seen with Jeffords, by appearing to be on friendly, or even more than friendly, terms with him. Her own hurt made her want to strike out at Clee, to hurt him as well.

Jeffords held a chair for her, and she sat down. Jeffords took a seat gingerly across from her and ruefully said: "I rode to the Vasquez and back several days ago, and I have not entirely recovered yet. When a man is not used to riding. . . ."

His expression deliberately invited her laughter, but she only smiled.

He was serious at once. He said, looking at her with eyes that were warmly personal, openly admiring: "Clee is a fool. If I had you to myself for as long as he had. . . ." He left the sentence unfinished, but his glance completed its meaning. Nan could feel herself flushing, could also feel a certain excitement rising within her.

Jeffords, with practiced ease, changed the direction of the conversation at once. He was a brilliant conversationalist. He made Nan forget her surroundings, almost made her forget Clee. His manner brought intimacy out of formality with no apparent effect. As he helped Nan to her feet at the conclusion of the meal, most of her revulsion was gone, all of her distrust. She even found herself liking Jeffords. And she was disturbed only slightly by the magnetic attraction he exerted against her.

Although she could not know it, this was his plain intent. He escorted her to her door, bowed gallantly, and left her with a very pleasant feeling, a certain regret at his leaving.

Going down the stairs, Jeffords smiled with complete satisfaction. Tonight had gone exactly as he had hoped it would. He was aware, however, that for this conquest he had very little time. The slow, sure approach would have to be abandoned, or short cut. He had only a little less than a week. Smiling, he thought it would be enough.

Chapter Twelve

With Clee Fahr at the reins, the buggy whirled north along the river road. The sky was gray, and a bitter wind shipped out of the north. Sibyl, modishly dressed in black, sat beside him. His face was solemn, sour with his own, growing self-disgust. He could not seem to forget that morning at the Massey cabin. He hated the memory of his clumsiness, but he could also feel a sort of resentful dismay because Nan had been so quick to misunderstand him. In going back over the night that had preceded the misunderstanding, he had began to realize ruefully that he'd had little or nothing to do with the things that had happened. Therefore, he should have felt absolved of blame. But he did not. He could only remember Nan, her sweetness, the wild excitement that had roared through him like a grass fire.

Sibyl broke his musing preoccupation, saying: "I'm leaving tomorrow, Clee."

Clee looked at her, pulling his thoughts away from Nan with an effort. The instant thought touched him: *She got the information she wanted from Levy. And Eames is ready.* He said, trying to adjust his thoughts to this new bit of information: "Leaving?"

Sibyl nodded, smiling. "Why don't you marry

her, Clee?" she asked. "She's right for you, as I never was."

He shrugged. "She won't have me."

"Nonsense. No woman could live in the same cabin with you as long as she has and not want you." There was an odd tremor in Sibyl's voice.

Clee laughed harshly. He could feel a liking growing up within himself for Sibyl, something he had never felt for her before. He asked: "Where are you going?"

Sibyl shrugged. "I don't know. Away from here to begin with. After that. . . ." She let her voice die.

Clee could see her utter despair in the sag of her shoulders, could hear it in the listlessness of her voice. He said angrily: "Damn Jeffords!"

"Eames has never. . . ." She looked at Clee's face. She saw his disbelief, his struggle against it. She murmured: "I'm lying, of course. You know it, and so do I. Now that I am going, there is no reason to hide it from you." She was pale, and Clee could see what it cost her to reveal this to him. She went on lifelessly. "After the duel they sent me to Louisiana to visit some cousins there. They said it was to spare me the scandal. Actually, it was to spare themselves. Eames followed me." Her face began to take on color. "Do you know . . . can you imagine how persuasive Eames can be, Clee? Do you know how damned attractive he is to women? Why are women such fools?" Her hand found his arm and clutched it. "Why does a man like that have such an attraction for a woman?"

Clee did not know, and said so. He wondered if Sibyl would betray Jeffords's plans, if he asked her to. He decided she might, also decided immediately that to ask her to would be the cruelest thing he could do to her.

"He told me he loved me, and I believed him, Clee. He did not mention marriage, but I thought nothing of that. I thought it was simply taken for granted in his mind as it was in mine. But I was wrong." Her voice dropped to a mere whisper. "By the time I found out that he had no intention of marrying me, it was too late."

Clee's jaw was hard. Anger boiled in his heart. He asked shortly: "Why didn't you quit him, then?"

Sibyl answered tonelessly: "I couldn't. If he had only possessed my body, it would have been easy. But he did more than that. He created a need in me for him, a need I couldn't seem to control. I hate him, Clee! I have since . . . well, since that first time, the time I realized that he had no intention of either marrying me or staying faithful to me. I have not liked myself, either, because I was unable to break away from him." She paused and stared at Clee. "Do you hate me for telling you this, Clee? I was going to keep it from you. I wanted you. But even when I wanted you, I wanted him, too."

Clee said uncomfortably: "I couldn't hate you, Sibyl."

She smiled. "Thank you, Clee."

He asked suddenly: "Why are you telling me this?"

"Because I can see how miserable you are. You've quarreled with Nanette. I can see that you want her. I don't want any lingering feeling you may have for me to spoil her for you."

Clee looked at her. She was desirable and lovely. He could sense that, in this one moment, she was his for the taking. He shrugged, and scowled, briefly hating his own uncompromising honesty that had lost him Nanette and now prevented him from taking Sibyl. Then he gave her a rueful smile. "Does a man ever understand a woman?"

"No, I guess he doesn't." Her eyes were soft, her lips full and unsmiling. She said, looking away from him: "Take me back now, Clee. I have got to finish my packing."

He turned the horse in the middle of the road. He felt an odd helplessness, and a sense of inadequacy. On the drive back, Sibyl kept the conversation on a strictly impersonal plane, but Clee's thoughts tended to speculation on Jeffords's plans. When he helped her alight before the Fremont House, she said: "I won't see you again, Clee. Would you kiss me good bye?"

He would have taken her in his arms, but she would not let him. She stood on tiptoe, planted a soft, warm kiss on his mouth. Then she was gone, her back to him as she ran up the steps to the hotel verandah. It seemed to Clee that she yanked open the door with unnecessary violence. She did not turn as she went through it, and Clee had the feeling that she was crying.

He jumped down and tied the buggy horse. He would have followed her, but a man blocked him on the walk, saying: "Got a match, Mister Fahr?"

Clee nodded, wary and at once on edge. The man was middle-aged, gray of hair and beard. His clothes were ragged and dirty, his hands horny and callused. *A miner,* thought Clee. The miner's eyes were brown, yet they were surprisingly hard, and they were careful eyes. "I want to talk to you," he said. "Sam said that you were the man to see."

Tension went abruptly out of Clee. He said: "Circle around to the rear of the Elephant Corral. I'll come out that way, after I've returned this buggy." He fished in his pocket, drew out a box of sulphur matches. He handed them to the man, waited while he puffed his pipe alight. Then he climbed back to the buggy seat.

The stranger shuffled into the alley behind the hotel. Clee drove downstreet and turned toward the Elephant Corral. His thoughts were churning. This must be one of the self-styled deserters Sam had planted on the Vasquez. He must have some sort of news. And Sibyl was leaving on tomorrow's stage. The two things fitted nicely together. Jeffords was ready, then.

Only briefly did Clee wonder whether the stage that would carry Sibyl would also carry the gold. He shook his head. No. It would be the one following that. Neither Jeffords nor Sibyl would chance complicating the robbery by her presence on the stage with the gold.

He swung down inside the corral and handed the reins to a hostler. He picked his way through the huge stable, toward the wide, rear door. It was almost dark in here, almost dark to a man whose eyes had so recently been blinded by afternoon sunlight. Clee felt a rising excitement.

A voice spoke to him from behind an old wagon. "Here, Mister Fahr." Clee's hand hovered an inch from the grip of his gun, and he advanced cautiously. The memory of another ambush was in him, and perhaps it was this memory that caused the odd tingle of uneasiness that traveled down his spine.

He came around the wagon, found the miner hunkered against a wagon wheel. The man was looking up, upward at something above Clee's head. Clee heard a slight rustle above him, and at the same instant the miner moved, diving forward against Clee's legs. Clee yanked the Colt, raised the barrel to deliver a blow against the miner's skull.

At that exact instant, the weight of a second man struck his neck and shoulders, as the man leaped upon him from the stable loft. Clee was driven forward, gun in hand, and his face connected violently with the hard-packed earthen floor. A heel ground down upon his wrist, and his finger involuntarily released the gun as sharp pain turned them numb.

The miner was clawing upward along his legs,

and Clee lashed out with his feet. He felt the sodden smash of heel against teeth, heard a pain-filled, vicious curse. He was fighting frantically now, but he was a good twenty pounds lighter than he had been upon his arrival in Denver several weeks before. The weight of the man jumping out of the loft had wrenched his wounded shoulder badly, and pain stabbed through it now. The miner caught the foot of his bad leg and twisted viciously.

With a part of his mind, Clee could think as he fought: *These aren't Sam's troopers. So they must be Jeffords's men. One of Sam's boys must have talked.* He squirmed convulsively, and half came to his knees. Something descended on the top of his head, and for the briefest instant it was as though his skull had been split wide open. Then everything was black.

Consciousness was fuzzy as it returned, almost unreal. Clee's head felt as though it were detached from his body, floating somewhere above it. He tried to raise a hand to it, discovered that he could not, and then felt the excruciating pain in his arms caused by lack of circulation. His wrists were bound together behind him, the ropes cruelly tight. Clee lay on his side, apparently in a wagon bed, for he could feel the rough, jolting movement of the vehicle.

He tried to brace his feet against the sides of the wagon, and discovered then that his ankles were also bound. A canvas, smelly and filthy, lay over him, entirely covering him. Through the cracks in the wagon bed beneath him, he looked down at the ground, flowing smoothly past. Cottonwood leaves in a rutted trail. Then the wagon was either following Cherry Creek or the Platte.

Clee's head began to throb. His scalp felt wet — probably from blood. The wagon crossed a small washout, and Clee's body bounced into the air, descended with a bone-jarring crash. He groaned. He heard a voice then. "Frank, he's comin' out of it. We almost there?"

The other man grunted. Clee judged that Frank was the man who had accosted him before the hotel. He had never gotten a glimpse of the second man.

He lay still now, hoping that by feigning unconsciousness he would be allowed to hear their talk. Frank said, speaking thickly, Clee judged, because of broken teeth and a bruised mouth: "I don't know why the hell Eames wouldn't let us just kill this one. Look at my mouth. Four front teeth gone. By God, they're beginning to hurt like hell, too."

"Fahr's a good friend of Massey's, that's why. You let his body be found, and some of Massey's troops are going to start smelling around."

"Hell, Jiggs, we wouldn't have to let him be found."

There was a certain cold quality suddenly in Jiggs's voice. "Eames is running this. Don't forget it. You ain't part of a penny-ante hold-up outfit now, you're part of an army. They hang men for goin' against orders."

There was a sour silence, broken only by the sound of Frank's spitting. The wagon jolted onward, and Clee rattled around in the bed of it, his body beating itself painfully against floor and sides. But at last it stopped, and he heard Jiggs's voice. "Here we are. Throw that canvas off him and help me lug him in."

Clee could feel hands fumbling with the canvas over him. It was flung back, and Clee looked up into Frank's face. Frank's lips were swelled and puffy. He glared at Clee, then spoke thickly over his shoulder. "Carry him, hell! He's awake. Let the bastard walk." He slipped a sheath knife from his belt and slashed Clee's feet free, staying well back from them as he did so, muttering: "By God, you kick me again, and I'll bury this knife in your belly."

Clee sat up. Clumsily he got to his knees, and on his knees crawled to the back of the wagon. He maneuvered himself into a sitting position on the foot-high end gate, and then slipped to the ground. He swayed, and his legs wobbled. Needles of pain ran up and down as blood pounded through them. He steadied himself against the wagon.

He looked at the cabin with a little surprise. Sam Massey's cabin. A wry grin touched his mouth. The perfect place to conceal him. Sam would be gone for at least two weeks, and by that time the stage and gold would be halfway to Texas. Nanette, having left the place, was not likely to return to it immediately.

Jiggs had gone in, and Clee could hear him poking around inside. Frank yielded to an irresistible desire for revenge. He said — "Go on, damn you." — and gave Clee a vicious shove.

Clee was off balance. His legs, due to an almost total lack of circulation for the past hour, would not support him. With his arms tied behind him, he fell heavily on his face. He tasted dirt and sand in his mouth. He rolled, spat, and sat up, glaring at Frank.

Frank laughed. The sun was down, and now the last pink glow faded from the westerly clouds. Gray dusk settled softly, bringing its early winter chill. Frank said unpleasantly: "If you can't walk, damn you, crawl."

Clee got to his knees. Once again, he struggled to his feet. He saw Frank moving in from the corner of one eye and swung to meet the man, his gray eyes murky and wild. Frank sought to shoulder him down, but Clee's knee came up into his crotch with a vicious thump. Clee fell, then, of course. His single leg would not support him.

Frank howled and bent double. Clee sat up again. Jiggs came hurrying out the door. "What the hell's going on out here?"

Clee said angrily: "Cut my hands loose and I'll break the rest of his teeth."

Jiggs grabbed him beneath the shoulders and hoisted him to his feet. He steadied Clee as he walked to the cabin. At the door, Clee flung a

backward glance at Frank. Complete viciousness was in the grizzled miner's hard, brown
eyes. His battered lips formed the word: "Wait."

Clee grinned at him, but there was no mirth in
the grin, nor was there mirth in this situation.
They would hold him here, under guard, until
the stage and its golden cargo were well away.
They had undoubtedly also seized Sam Massey's
lookouts at the Vasquez.

Clee sat down at the table. Jiggs poked around
in the stove, getting a fire started, and, when
Frank slouched through the door, he said: "Take
that bucket and get some water."

Frank scowled with surly ill-humor, but he
picked up the bucket and went out.

Jiggs came around behind Clee and looked at
his bound wrists. He said: "I'll untie these for a
few minutes, if you'll promise not to try anything."

Clee said: "I'll promise, but only temporarily."

"Good enough." A knife slashed through the
ropes. Clee brought the arms around in front of
him. Excruciating pain shot through them from
the fingers clear to his shoulders. He began to
chafe them gingerly. He asked: "One of Sam's
men talked?"

Jiggs nodded. He was a big man, with a hollow,
boy face and tremendous, long arms. His brows
were bushy, his nose long and hooked. His eyes
were a penetrating blue and were sunken far into
their sockets, giving him the appearance of a
man who was ill. Jiggs said: "He got drunk and

142

dropped a hint. Some of the boys slapped him around, and he spilled the whole story. So we grabbed the other two Sam had up there. Then we came down and grabbed you. Now our plan will go off without a hitch." He considered Clee for a moment, finally saying: "You made a mistake with Frank. He'll make it rough on you, when I'm gone."

Clee shrugged. His head was throbbing mercilessly, and, as the blood poured back into his arms, they began to burn. His mind rummaged ceaselessly through the things he knew, at last coming to the one inevitable conclusion as he had known it would. Jeffords had covered every loophole. And unless Clee himself could escape, the seizure of the stage would proceed with ridiculous ease.

Frank came back and banged the bucket down atop the stove. His muttered obscenities were plainly audible to both Clee and Jiggs, when he saw Clee's unbound wrists. He said: "Jeffords said to keep him tied."

"He's got to eat, don't he? You want to feed him?"

Frank shrugged. There was nothing but pain and hopelessness in Clee. He could recognize that escape was an impossibility. Physically he was no match for either of these men of Jeffords. Not in his present condition. And they both had weapons, while he had none.

He hobbled over to the bed and lay down. He thought of Nanette, of Sibyl, of Sam Massey.

Gradually, very gradually, determination replaced his hopelessness. Nothing could be done tonight. He was too weak from the blow he had taken on the head. But tomorrow . . . ? He shrugged, and closed his eyes.

Chapter Thirteen

Wednesday passed uneventfully, as did Thursday and Friday. On Saturday, Jiggs mounted his horse and set out for the mountains to kill a deer. Clee, hands bound behind him, stood at the tiny window and watched him go. Frank stood at the door. When Jiggs had passed from sight in the bare-stripped cottonwoods, Frank turned.

His eyes, singularly hard in his bearded face, seemed to hold a sort of secret pleasure. Clee thought: *Now he'll pay me off for smashing his teeth.*

Frank's lips had healed somewhat, until now he could hold a wheatstraw cigarette between them. The jagged stumps of his teeth pained him terribly, kept him awake at night, cursing. Frank said sourly: "Two more days. Two more days to live, bucko." His eyes had an odd glitter as he approached Clee. He said: "Sit down in that chair."

Clee shook his head. "To hell with you."

Frank came in with a rush. His right, solidly swung, grazed the side of Clee's jaw, nearly tearing his ear off. His left buried itself in Clee's middle. Clee strained at the ropes that bound his hands, strained uselessly. Off balance, he staggered back across the room. He piled into the table, overturned it, and caught himself on its

145

rim with his hands, so securely bound behind him.

Growling deeply in his throat, Frank followed. He was a squat and solid man, thick of shoulder and chest. Clee flung his head to one side, and Frank's blow missed. His own momentum flung him against Clee, and Clee's knee came up, missing his groin, catching him in the belly. Frank grunted as the wind drove out of him.

With both hands, he pushed himself away. He backed off, his breath sucking in and out of his lungs with a sound like a bellows. Now there was pure murder in his slitted eyes.

He stood, breathing hard, while the color returned to his face, while his starving lungs drank air. Then he moved toward Clee again.

A voice spoke from the open doorway, an amused, pleased voice. "I thought it was a waste of time to come out here today. Now I see that it wasn't. Proceed, Frank, but let's not make it too quick. I'm thoroughly enjoying this."

Clee looked around. Eames Jeffords stood in the door, shoulder point against its jamb, smoking a long, black cigar. His lips were smiling beneath the long mustache, but his eyes were not. They were hot with pleasure, with sadistic anticipation. Frank had stopped, hands dangling, utterly surprised and taken aback. Jeffords said, perhaps a little sharply: "Go on, Frank. Go on."

Frank began to grin. He said, wetting his lips: "I thought you was Jiggs. He wouldn't like this."

"No, I'm not Jiggs." There was poorly concealed impatience in Jeffords's voice.

Frank came in, a little crouched. He swung a right at Clee's mouth that would have filled it with broken teeth. Clee ducked slightly, and the fist skidded off the top of his head. But Frank's left caught him in the groin, doubling him over with its sharp pain. The right again connected high on his cheekbone.

Helpless rage was born in Clee. Jeffords suggested from the door: "Mark his face up."

Clee's fury mounted. Blood pounded in his temples. He gritted his teeth. As Frank's next blow started, Clee wove to one side, then drove headlong at Frank's midsection. His head thudded viciously against Frank's chest, pushing him back. Frank tripped and fell. As Clee fell on top of him, Frank's knee drove full into Clee's face. Blood spurted from his nose. He rolled aside, trying to avoid Frank's thrashing feet, but one of the man's heavy boots caught him in the throat. Choking, gasping, Clee tried to come to his knees. Frank was up before him, and cuffed him viciously on the side of the head. Clee went to the floor.

He saw Frank's boot draw back, and tried to roll. He was too late. Frank's foot slammed against his back with a force that should have broken his spine. But the foot struck both of Clee's hands, tied behind his back. Clee grabbed, even as the pain lashed so fiercely from the hands. He felt the toe of Frank's boot in one hand, and gripped hard. His other hand slipped up, got a higher hold on the boot.

Frank jerked his foot, but he was off balance, and there was little power in the tug against Clee's clutching hands. Still holding on, Clee rolled toward him. Frank crashed down on top of him.

Clee rolled out from under, immediately coming to his knees. Clee had nothing with which to strike, save for his head. So he drove against Frank, and felt his head connect with the man's hard chin.

Pain and this towering rage were so intermingled in Clee that he had forgotten Jeffords altogether. Now Jeffords stepped forward and kicked Clee in the side. He kicked again. Clee rolled off Frank, trying to get to Jeffords, and, as he rolled, Jeffords kicked him in the belly.

Consciousness was slipping away from Clee. His eyes were swelling, and filled with blood from a deep cut on his forehead. His nose ran a steady stream of blood. He lay on his side in a crouched position, trying to protect his belly from those vicious kicks. He saw Frank stumble groggily to his feet.

He knew he was being a fool. He had no chance in this. If, by some freakish mischance, he happened to down Frank, then there was still Jeffords. And while Jeffords would disdain the use of his fists in a fight, he would undoubtedly use his feet, or the long barrel of his pistol.

Clee knew he had never hated anything or

anyone quite so intensely as he hated Jeffords at this moment. Frank shook his shaggy head and came on once more. He was like a wounded animal in his utter and complete rage.

Jeffords spoke sharply: "Stop it, Frank!"

Frank paid him no attention. He drew back a boot to kick at Clee. Jeffords came across the room in one rapid stride. His revolver barrel slashed at Frank, raking a furrow across his brow. Jeffords said again, his voice like the pop of a whip: "Stop it! God damn you, do what I tell you to do."

Frank stood like a whipped dog, head down, trembling.

Jeffords said: "Go outside and wash the blood off you. I want to talk to Clee."

He waited until Frank went out the door, until he heard the crashing passage of the man through the brush that lined the creek. Pride was all that brought Clee struggling to his knees. Twice he fell back, but on the third try he made it to his feet. He walked to the bed and sat down.

Jeffords was smiling, a steady, mocking smile. He asked: "What did you do to Nanette Massey? Up until she moved into town, she would have nothing to do with me." His smile widened. "Now I find her very friendly. Perhaps she is interested in a comparison."

Clee scowled. Rage had burned itself out in him. Now there was only hate, cold, implacable hate. He said: "If you touch her, I'll kill you."

Jeffords laughed aloud. "What an idle threat.

How do you expect to accomplish that? Your hands are tied. You could not even whip Frank. The day after tomorrow I will be gone, headed for Texas with forty men and a quarter million in gold. And you'll be dead."

He took a fresh cigar from his pocket, bit off the end, and lighted it. He blew the fragrant smoke at Clee. He murmured regretfully: "It's a damned shame, when you have to rush a woman. I would have preferred to take my time with Nanette." He shrugged expressively. "Unfortunately, that wasn't possible. I must leave Denver Monday. But I think she is ready. I think perhaps tonight. . . ."

Clee lunged up from the bed. Frank came through the door, fiercely scowling. He held a hand across his mouth. He said: "God, Lieutenant, send someone out here from Denver to pull these teeth. They're driving me crazy."

Clee halted his lunging passage across the room. He would be in no position even to attempt escape if he let them beat him any more. Jeffords, from the door, asked: "Tell me, Clee, is Nanette really worth a man's time and trouble?"

It was no longer hate that whirled in Clee's brain. It was madness. Frank came across the room and shoved him back onto the bed. Frank cuffed him viciously across the mouth.

Jeffords went to the door. "Nanette will be expecting me. I'll give her your regards." He went outside. Clee got up and crossed to the door. If he only had the use of his hands! He strained against the ropes, strained and twisted until he tore the flesh from his wrists. He felt blood running down his hands.

Jeffords mounted his horse and rode over to the door. He affected sincere puzzlement. He said: "You know, Clee, women are funny creatures. A man never knows when they say no whether they mean it or not. Sometimes I think a little force. . . ." He laughed, and dug his heels into the horse's sides. He rode out of the clearing, at its edge looking back, white teeth flashing in a mocking smile.

Frank said: "Now I can finish what I started."

Clee stood utterly motionless, looking at him. His eyes were a murky gray, as cold and hard as slate. He murmured softly: "If you lay a hand on me again, you had better kill me. Because you'll regret it, if you don't."

Something about the certainty in those gray eyes of Clee's must have halted Frank. His clubbed fist stopped in mid-air. He muttered something beneath his breath, but he turned away. Clee sat down at the table.

Surly and grumbling, Frank went over to the stove, stirred around in the ashes, and added some wood. He poured some water into the coffee pot and set it on the front of the stove. Then he returned and lashed a rope around Clee's body and the back of the chair. He knotted it, and then went over and lay down on the bed.

With quiet desperation, Clee thought of

Nanette. He thought of Sibyl's words describing the attraction Jeffords had for women. He thought of Nanette, tight in Jeffords's arms. Fury heated his body, and he began to sweat.

He admitted that he loved Nanette. But what can a man do when a woman refuses him? At last, he thought of Jeffords's threat to use force on Nanette tonight. He stirred in the chair, edged it as silently as he could a foot toward the stove, watching Frank.

Frank opened his eyes. He said softly: "Go on. I've been waiting for you to try it."

Clee relaxed in the chair. He was not doubting that eventually he would get his chance. But would he get it soon enough? He doubted if he would.

Chapter Fourteen

Jiggs returned at dusk, a deer slung across the saddle before him. He called to Frank from the door — "Come on out and skin this critter." — and dismounted, coming at once into the cabin.

He poured a wash pan full of warm water from the stove and washed the blood and tallow from his hands. He looked across at Clee, squinting in the lamplight. He saw the cuts, the dried blood, the blue-black bruises on Clee's face. He said: "I ought to turn you loose and let you have at him. Damn a man that will use his fist on someone that can't fight back." He came around behind Clee and untied the ropes that bound Clee to the chair. He asked: "If I untie your hands, will you give me your parole?"

Clee shook his head.

"Don't be a fool! You can't get away. You had just as well be as comfortable as you can."

Clee was wondering why he didn't give his parole with tongue in cheek and break it at the first opportunity that presented itself. He knew he might have done that with Frank, for there was no honor in Frank at all. Jiggs was different. He had tried to be decent with Clee, and Clee could not reward him with treachery. Besides, he told himself, he would receive no thanks from Nanette for interfering in her affairs. He had asked her to marry him, and she had refused. And that was that. Her life was her own.

Jiggs built up the fire. Frank brought in a quarter of venison, and Jiggs sliced off some steaks, put them on to fry. When supper was ready, he put it on the table. He untied Clee's hands, stepping back at once and drawing his revolver. He said: "You and Frank eat. If you won't give me your parole, I'll have to keep a gun on you."

Clee stood up, swinging his arms, trying to restore circulation in them. He chafed his arms and hands, wincing every time he touched his raw and bleeding wrists. His hands felt like huge clubs, and he could hardly move his fingers. His head ached furiously from the beating he had received this afternoon. When he picked up a knife to cut his meat, he found that he could not hold it. So he picked up the piece of meat in his hand and tore at it with his teeth.

He ate two pieces of meat and gulped a cup of scalding coffee. Holding the heavy coffee mug, he glanced at Jiggs out of the corner of his eye, gauging his chances. He looked back at Frank, found the man watching him with gleeful anticipation. He put the coffee mug back on the table and stood up. Jiggs was alert, a gun in his hand. Frank was only hoping Clee would begin something.

He went back over and sat down again in the chair. Jiggs tossed his gun to Frank, and then proceeded to tie him again. Perhaps it was pity for Clee's lacerated wrists that made him draw the ropes less tightly than they had been before.

Clee looked around the cabin. It was a shambles. He remembered how tidy and clean Nanette had kept it. Jiggs sat at the table, eating. When he had finished, he shoved the dishes to one end, got out a dog-eared deck of cards, and began to play solitaire. The hours dragged.

Clee was recalling how it had been that last night with Nanette. He was remembering the weeks of patient care she had given him, the easy comradeship which had sprung up between them during that time. Perhaps even now she was in Jeffords's arms, willing and ardent. Or perhaps Jeffords had found it necessary to use force. Slow, intolerable rage burned in Clee. He began to work at the ropes that bound his hands. The pain brought beads of sweat to his face.

Jiggs cocked an eye at him. He said: "It's no use, Clee. You're tied good. You're just hurtin' yourself for nothin'." He yawned and stood up. He untied the rope that held Clee to the chair, and bent to examine the ropes on Clee's wrists. He said: "Go lie down on the bed. I'll have to tie your feet, too."

Frank sat on the floor in the far corner of the room, a whiskey bottle between his knees. At intervals, he would raise it to his lips, take a drink. Each time he did, his face contorted as the fiery liquor bit into the nerve ends of his shattered teeth. Yet each time he drank, the pain was apparently less. He was getting thoroughly drunk.

155

Jiggs looked at him and grunted disgustedly. "Looks like I'm the one to stay awake tonight."

Clee lay on his bed, and Jiggs roped his feet together. Exhaustion was an insistent pressure on Clee. He wondered if his chance would come tonight. He doubted it. For one thing, he was helpless with the use of neither his arms nor legs. For another, he was dead for sleep. He needed to be fresh for the ordeal that lay ahead.

His thoughts kept straying to Nanette, but each time they did, he forced them to something else, closing his mind to all thought of her. He counted off the days Sam Massey had been gone, speculating as to whether or not it was possible that Sam might return unexpectedly. He decided it was not possible. Nor would Clee be missed at the Fremont House. Nanette would not miss him, indeed, could not be expected to know whether he was in Denver or not. Sibyl might have missed him, but Sibyl was gone.

In the last analysis, he could depend upon no one but himself. Determinedly, he composed his thoughts, and at last went to sleep.

Sunday was no different from the other endless days of captivity, except that Clee knew it was his last. Jiggs was more vigilant even than usual, sensing perhaps that, if Clee made a break, it would come today.

In late afternoon, Jiggs left Frank on guard and went into the lean-to to sleep. Frank sat at the table, a short cigar in his battered mouth, the last bottle of whiskey half empty on the table before him. Clee gave Jiggs what he judged to be half an hour to go to sleep. Then he said: "I've got to go outside, Frank."

Frank scowled at him. He seemed half on the point of refusing, but at last he got up and came across the room to where Clee sat, bound to the chair. Clee had been tightening the knots of the rope that bound his hands all afternoon in anticipation of this, straining endlessly at the ropes, allowing them to become soaked and slippery with blood.

Frank untied the rope that bound Clee to the chair. He fumbled at the knots that tied Clee's hands unsuccessfully, cursing softly. At last, as Clee had known the man would, Frank yanked his knife from its sheath and cut the ropes. Clee stood up, making no move toward him, carefully rubbing his arms to restore circulation.

Frank growled: "No tricks now, damn you. Go on outside."

Clee went through the door. The sky was overcast, and a light, cold wind blew out of the north. He shivered, as he went across the clearing and into the trees, Frank close behind, gun in hand.

A few minutes later, the two came out of the trees again and returned to the cabin. Clee was careful to make no overt move, to do nothing that might arouse Frank's suspicion. He went inside and sat down again in the chair. Frank picked up the rope that lay on the floor, the one which had previously been used only to lash Clee to the back of the chair.

Clee obligingly held his hands behind him. He gritted his teeth, for he knew how this would be. Frank would be as cruel as he could about it. But Clee was hoping Frank would tie him as he had done more than once before. Frank was always nervous, being this close to Clee. He was always afraid that Clee would whirl on him, exact terrible revenge for the abuse Frank had given him the day Jeffords had visited the cabin. So whenever he had to tie Clee, he always tied his body to the back of the chair first, winding the rope around and around, then proceeding to tie the hands with the other, shorter piece of rope.

Today, Clee was counting on this, and he was not disappointed. With the longer rope wound around and around Clee's body and the chair back, Frank turned to look for the other piece, then remembered that he had been forced to cut it. Grumbling, he proceeded to tie Clee's hands with the two ends of the longer rope, pulling them tight with unnecessary viciousness and knotting them tight. Clee could scarcely conceal his satisfaction, although the pain from his wrists turned him dizzy and cold.

Frank looked at his face, pale from the pain, and laughed. Then he returned to the table and tipped the bottle to his mouth. He said: "This is your last night, bucko. You want a little drink?"

"I could use one."

Frank sloshed liquor into a glass. He carried it over to Clee. Suddenly he drew back his hand

and dashed it into Clee's face. Clee gasped, blinked his eyes against the sting of the alcohol.

Jiggs came in, rubbing sleep from his eyes. His face turned dark with anger, when he saw Clee's helpless attempts to clear his eyes. He walked across the room and yanked the bottle from Frank. "Damn you, if I have to be around you much more, I'm going to kill you. You ain't fit to live with since you broke those teeth."

"Since *he* broke them!" Frank gestured angrily at Clee. He went on, whining: "I asked Lieutenant Jeffords to send a man out here to pull them for me. But he hasn't done it. I wonder . . . does he think a man can ride all the way to Texas like this?"

"You know where you could get them pulled?" asked Jiggs.

"Sure. There's an old dentist that lives in a shack under the McGaa Street bridge. I could slip up the creek bottom, if you'd keep your mouth shut about it."

Jiggs shrugged. "All right. But don't let anyone see you, especially not Eames Jeffords. And no more liquor . . . you understand?"

"Sure, Jiggs. Sure." Frank slipped on his ragged coat, fumbling from habit for the buttons that weren't there. Finally, holding the coat about him, he stepped outside.

Jiggs went over and kicked the door shut. There was a certain nervousness in him. He said: "Big day tomorrow."

Clee did not answer. He was calculating the

time he had, the time that would be allowed to him before Frank returned. Jiggs turned toward the stove to pull the coffee pot toward the front of it. While his back was turned, Clee leaned silently against the ropes that bound him to the chair back. They gave but slightly, and they made the slightest of creaking noises as his weight bore against them.

Tentatively he brought his hands upwards, at the same time raising his body. He felt the ropes slip ever so slightly up the chair's smooth back. This was his chance, the thing he had hoped and planned for. If he could get but a short instant, he could stand up, thus raising the chair from the floor. By wiggling his body and his bound arms, he thought he could get the chair to slip down, out of the ropes entirely. This would create enough slack in the ropes so that Clee could unwind them from about his wrists. It might even give him enough to slip them free without even untying the knots.

Once free, he had two alternatives, one of which was to attack and either kill or stun Jiggs. The other was flight. For the second alternative, darkness would be a requirement. And the second alternative appealed to Clee the most. For one thing, until circulation returned to his arms and hands, he would hardly be adept at handling any weapon.

Then he needed two things: darkness and something to pull Jiggs away from the cabin, if only for a few short minutes. Darkness, he calculated looking at the graying window, was perhaps thirty minutes away. He guessed that Frank would be back in about an hour, so the time he would have after dark fell would be something less than thirty minutes.

Jiggs poured himself a cup of coffee and sat, sipping it. Apparently remembering Clee, he asked: "Cup of coffee? I'll untie you for a minute, if you want some."

Clee shook his head. Jiggs got the deck of cards, spread them out on the table, and began to play solitaire. The minutes sped past. Light faded in the window until it was entirely black. Clee asked: "Which one of you has Eames got picked out to kill me?"

Jiggs would not look at him. Clee could see that he hated this part of it. In other circumstances, Clee knew he would have liked this cadaverous man. Jiggs muttered: "Frank."

Clee knew that Frank would relish the job. He also knew that Frank would have to use more than one bullet. He'd give it to Clee in the belly first, just to see him suffer.

Impatience built intolerably in Clee. Another half hour passed. Frank would be coming back any time now. Jiggs seemed to have the same idea, for he stopped his game and went to the window to peer uselessly through it.

Clee knew his plan of escape was out now. There would be no flight. He had noticed Jiggs, fidgeting on the bench at the table, had hoped the man would soon be forced to go outside. His heart leaped as Jiggs said: "I got to go outside for a minute." It was all Clee could do to show indifference.

Jiggs glanced at him once, then went to the door. A blast of cold air struck Clee as he opened it. Clee thought desperately: *Shut it, damn you! Shut it!* He said irritably: "For Christ's sake, shut that door. It's cold."

The blast of cold air ceased. Clee shot a lightning glance over his shoulder at the door. Jiggs was gone.

Swiftly, trembling at his knees, Clee came to his feet. He wriggled violently. The chair slipped perhaps an inch, then stopped as the ropes drew tighter and caught. Clee hunched his shoulders, drawing them together. How long would Jiggs stay out? The answer to that was easy. No longer than he had to. It was cold, and he had taken no coat.

He wriggled again, and the chair slipped again. Clee's desperate thoughts cried: *It won't work. I've taken too long already.*

Violently he contorted his body, clawed with his hands at the back of the chair, trying to force it down, out of the ropes. He knew he should be calm, knew this frantic hurry was only slowing things down. He drew his shoulders together, and worked them up and down. With a crash, the chair fell out, and struck the floor. Immediately there was slack, precious slack.

Knowing that he was probably already too late, Clee crossed the room, searching for a weapon. There was none. Everything that could be used as a weapon having been removed by Jiggs's foresight. His eye fell upon the woodbox.

Meanwhile, he had been straining at the ropes, working his hands. He heard a step on the board stoop outside the door, heard the creak of the door's leather hinges.

Too late! Too late! His hands came free, numb and bleeding. He tried to pick up a heavy stick of firewood, but his fingers would not close around it. He knew a moment of panic.

With both hands then, he gripped a stick of wood, a heavy, knotty one. Faintly he heard a shout, distantly, from the direction of Denver. He heard Jiggs's sour curse outside the half-open door. "Damn him! I told him no liquor."

Jiggs had not come in. Frank's drunken shout had held him outside the door for the precious instant Clee needed. Clee stationed himself behind the door. He was banking on another thing now. The cabin was too small to conceal the fact that he was no longer bound in his chair from anyone opening the door from outside. Clee was betting on a man's instinctive reaction to seeing something amiss. Jiggs would leap forward into the room. And Clee would be right behind him.

Softly cursing, Jiggs remained outside. Frank's voice came closer, and now he began to sing.

Clee realized that Jiggs might well stay outside until Frank reached the cabin. If that happened, he was lost. His fingers were beginning to tingle now, and pain lashed in both directions from his wrists. But he could feel again with his hands. He could feel the roughness of the stick he held. As far as they would, he let his fingers curl around the stick.

Panic again stirred him. He called: "Damn it, come in or go out. But shut the door."

Jiggs came in. For an instant there was utter silence in the cabin. Then he jumped aside and slammed the door. He was facing Clee. His hand curled around his gun butt. His mouth opened to shout.

Then Clee was on him. The strength and speed of desperation were in his driving legs. With the chunk of wood upraised, he crossed to Jiggs before the man could back up or step aside. The sound of his blow against Jiggs's forehead was solid and dull.

Jiggs's eyes glazed. Clee stooped as he fell and wrenched the gun from his limp fingers. Then he flung open the door and stepped out into the bitter wind. Frank's singing could be no more than a hundred feet away. Clee closed the door behind him and began to walk silently across the clearing. He saw the square of light as the door flung open, saw Frank's body silhouetted against the light.

Then he was running, with no regard for noise. Frank was drunk. So he had a little time, at least, until Jiggs could be revived. By that time he could be in the clear. Or so he hoped.

Chapter Fifteen

Clee bore north, skirting the encampment of plains Indians. Their dogs came out and barked at his heels, but he went on, knowing that in speed alone lay his chance of escape. The wind whirled out of the north, carrying a damp, frosty smell, and Clee knew that before long it would be snowing. The sky was utterly black, with no stars showing through the thick layer of cloud.

Cooking fires winked in the Indians' camp. He could see their darkly silhouetted bodies against the flickering orange light. He was shivering violently, utterly chilled, as he came into the scattering shacks that marked the westerly limits of the town. He headed at once for the old Antelope House where Massey's troop was quartered. A sentry, stationed there more for the purpose of keeping the troop in rather than keeping others out, stood before the door.

Clee's teeth were chattering with cold as he asked: "Champion here?"

The sentry stared at him, shaking his head.

Clee felt a certain impatience. He asked: "Know where you can find him?"

"Sure. He's uptown."

"Get him, will you? It's important."

The sentry stared for just another moment.

165

Then he stuck his head in the door and bawled: "Cawpril o' the guard!"

Another trooper, blouseless, in red, long-sleeved underwear, laid down his paper and sauntered to the door. Clee pushed past the sentry and went in. The warmth hit him like a blow, but he could not stop shivering. He walked over to the stove, standing red-hot in the center of the lobby.

Feeling had returned to his arms, and the pain from his wrists, intensified by the cold, was terrible. He held them out for the trooper to see. "I've been tied up for four days at Sam Massey's cabin. The Rebs are planning to grab the stage tomorrow. There's a quarter million in gold going East on it. Send a man uptown after Champion, will you?"

The corporal of the guard slid a chair across the floor to him, and Clee sat down. Then the man bawled an order, and shortly an orderly came running. The corporal sent him after Champion.

He went out back to the commissary, and returned a few moments later with a tin cup filled to the brim with whiskey. "Man, you need something like this. Drink it down."

Troopers crowded into the bare lobby, milling around Clee. What had once been a hotel dining room across the lobby had been converted into a barracks, and the walls were lined with cots. Troopers crowded curiously in its doorway. Clee felt exhaustion claiming him. The whiskey was fiery, but it warmed his body. He began to feel drowsy.

Lieutenant Champion came in, not recognizing Clee until Clee told him his name. Clee spilled his story swiftly, and, when he had finished, Champion was brisk and authoritative. To the corporal he said: "Take Mister Fahr to my quarters. Then call the troop in here." To Clee he said: "Get yourself some sleep. I'll send the surgeon up right away to see what he can do for those wrists of yours."

Clee climbed the stairs wearily. He allowed the surgeon to bandage his wrists. Then he fell back, exhausted, on the bed. He was instantly asleep.

The stage rolled at ten. The gold was inside on the floor in four, iron-bound chests. A shotgun guard rode beside the driver, and there were two passengers inside the coach. Champion had wanted to alert both Levy and the driver, had wanted to replace the passengers with a pair of his troopers. Clee had held out against him, knowing that at the slightest sign of resistance, every man in and on the coach would be killed.

The snow, which Clee had expected last night, now began to materialize. Tiny, stinging flakes whipped along on the wind, which was cold and raw. Dust whirled up from beneath the coach's wheels and rolled ahead of the four, trotting horses.

A trooper, who had watched the gold loaded, slipped down the alley and got his horse from between two buildings. He headed out of town at a dead run a quarter mile ahead of the stage, quartering away from the road toward the low line of hills to the westward.

Five miles from town, at the crest of a low knoll, Clee and Lieutenant Champion squatted, smoking and peering into the haze of snow that drove steadily from the northeast. Behind them, hidden from sight by the knoll itself, were thirty troopers, standing by their mounts.

Fierce anticipation and excitement stirred in Clee, excitement that had nothing to do with gold. Today, if things went right, he could come at last to grips with Eames Jeffords. There could be no backing down today in Jeffords.

Champion, a slight, dark-haired man of about thirty, knocked the ash of his cigar thoughtfully. "You have no idea how many men will be involved in this, nor where they will strike?"

Clee shook his head. "Eames has been buying guns. Sam thought he might have thirty or forty men."

Champion dragged a heavy silver watch from his pocket. "Ten-thirty," he said. "They ought to be along pretty soon."

The road lay before them, a mile away. Clee stared downward through the thickening snow. The road was invisible now. He said: "We had better close in a little. The stage could pass without us seeing it."

Champion nodded. He stood up and moved back toward his men. Clee heard the drum of hoofs faintly in the distance. He ran for his horse and swung to his saddle. Digging in his spurs, he raced out to intercept the rider.

Sounds were oddly muffled by the snow, and the soft, jingling sounds of the troop in movement behind him came only dimly to Clee. At a gallop, the rider passed, and Clee swung in behind, spurring his horse. There was sudden silence ahead. Clee pulled in, slowing his horse to a walk. He drew his Colt revolver and moved ahead into the blinding, whirling snow. He saw the shadowy form of horse and rider ahead, and the man's voice came softly out of the storm: "Lieutenant?"

"I'm Fahr. Lieutenant Champion is right behind me."

The man kicked his mount and rode close to Clee. He said: "The gold is on the stage, and they're right behind me." Snow was crusted on the front of his uniform, on his bushy brows and beard, and had frozen into cakes of ice. His face was red. Clee whirled the horse, saying — "Come on, then." — and rode back until he could see the shadowy forms of the troop, ahead of him and moving slowly toward the road. The trooper he had intercepted rode into the group and reported to Champion.

They were in the road, before they realized they had reached it. Champion muttered to Clee: "This is going to be pure hell. You can't see fifty feet ahead of you." To his men, he shouted: "Get off the road far enough so that you can just see me. After the coach passes, we'll have to fall in behind. Wait for me to give you the word before you close in."

Clee was suddenly glad he had insisted that no troopers be stationed inside the coach, for today it would be totally impossible to prevent the robbery of the coach. The most they could possibly expect to accomplish would be to interfere and retake it from the Confederate forces.

The troopers rode away from the road, halting and forming shadowy, indistinct groups. Clee followed Champion as he rode to join one of them. In a matter of minutes, the driving snow had obliterated tracks from the road. The horses fidgeted, and the men swore softly. Chill crept through their soaked coats, and snow soaked through their trouser legs.

For what seemed an eternity they waited. Once Champion called to the man who had preceded the stage, asking: "How far behind you were they?"

"A quarter mile when I left town. I cut across country and maybe gained a little."

Clee said: "Weather's bad. They'll be traveling slower than usual."

Another quarter hour passed. At last, the long shout of the stage driver rolled toward them, and then they could hear the squeak of bullhide springs, the jangle of harness. The shadowy, huge shape of the coach passed on the road. Champion's voice was muffled: "Come on."

They reached the road, and the other group,

seeing them, joined them at once. Already the stage was out of sight in the driving snow. But its tracks remained, quickly being drifted over with snow. Champion set out at the head of the troop, riding at a fast trot.

When the wheel tracks in the road would dim, he would increase his pace. When they grew overly sharp and clearly defined, he would reduce it. This way, they covered nearly ten miles.

There was no let-up in the storm. The troopers began to grumble and to cast questioning, doubtful glances at Clee. He knew what they were thinking. They were blaming him because they were out here, soaking wet in this storm. They were beginning to doubt if the stage would be seized at all.

Even Champion seemed to have lost his former assurance. Clee, still weak from the beating he had received, was shivering violently.

The road began to climb now, twisting and turning as it did to reduce the grade. Scrub cedars appeared on right and left. A bunch of antelope raced along, shadowy and unreal, paralleling the road.

Champion growled — "Hell, I doubt . . . !" — but he was interrupted by a violent flurry of shots from ahead. They were strangely muffled by the snow curtain that hung between the stage and Massey's troop.

Champion raised an arm. At once, with no confusion and no more doubt, the command split evenly, one group with Champion leaving the road to circle right up the slope, the other with Clee turning left. Clee sunk his spurs in his horse's ribs. Snow lay six inches deep on the clay slope. His horse skidded, and Clee was forced to slow him to a canter.

Almost silently, they swept forward through an unreal world of gray-white. Clee was not thinking of gold, or of the War Between the States. He was thinking of Eames Jeffords, whose evil influence had been over all his life, who had ruined Sibyl, who, quite possibly, had. . . . He blocked his mind to that thought. Yet he knew the power Jeffords had over women, particularly ones who were young and inexperienced. Perhaps even now Nanette was as much Jeffords's slave as Sibyl had ever been.

A red haze drifted across his vision. He stood in his stirrups, suddenly yelling. And at that instant they burst into view of the Rebels.

Clee leveled his revolver and fired. A man tumbled from his horse, and the animal bucked off down the slope, reins trailing. Clee's troopers had fanned out behind him, and now their fire blossomed pale orange in the dim gray of the heavy snow.

They had the advantage of complete surprise. Clee did not know it, but neither Jiggs nor Frank had found the courage to confess their failure to Jeffords. Jeffords thought Clee was dead. Only the impenetrability of the storm had persuaded Jeffords to throw his entire force against the coach. He had been afraid of their becoming separated unless he did.

The first wave of attack forced the Rebels back, back away from the coach. They apparently did not know that only fifteen men were in the attacking party. Then, as they retreated, Lieutenant Champion hit them from the other side. In the first flurry of shots, Clee's troopers had emptied four saddles. Champion's attack emptied three.

The coach driver, perceiving his chance, and his danger if he remained, popped his whip viciously over the backs of his teams, and the ponderous vehicle began to roll. No shot had been fired from the coach, and none was fired now.

As the coach rolled past him, Clee saw the shotgun guard up on the box, his gun idly resting across his knees. The white faces of the two passengers peered at him briefly from the window.

Champion's force had driven the Rebels off the road, down a long draw. The side of the hill steepened, and a horse fell. The rider, pinned beneath the animal, struck by the flying hoofs, screamed with pain. Clee yelled — "Come on." — to the scattered and hesitant troopers, and spurred his horse recklessly downhill.

He wished the snow were not so thick. He could hardly distinguish between friend and foe, let alone pick Eames Jeffords from the milling, retreating Rebels.

His gun was empty. He lifted the reins, held them in his teeth while he slipped out the cylinder, replaced it with a loaded spare he carried in his pocket. A bullet plucked his hat from his head. Snow stung his eyes, melted, and ran across his face. His horse shied as a bullet burned its hip. The Rebels, on a slightly level spot, halted at someone's shouted order, and formed a line. Clee saw Champion, riding full tilt, driven backward limply from his saddle.

Champion had been in the lead. The whole troop saw him fall. Clee perceived the instant hesitation in them. He stood in his stirrups and waved his Colt. "God damn you!" he yelled. "You wanted a fight. Now you got one. Give 'em hell! Give 'em bloody hell!" He swept ahead, and, when they saw him, their hesitation vanished.

The Rebs had no chance to attack. Clee's screaming thirty were on them, firing at point-blank range, crowding the Rebels back by the weight and power of their charge. Horses crashed together, and reared, screaming. A voice yelled — "Enough! Enough!" — and the yell was choked off as a ball caught the man in the throat.

But the cry had been heard, and it was taken up. The Rebels flung their weapons away, flung their arms above their heads. Clee yelled: "All right! Take prisoners!"

A yelling, confused tangle. Clee was looking for but one man, feeling a rising, murderous anger that he was to be thus deprived of his chance to face Eames Jeffords and kill him. Surrender! Jeffords would surrender, and again Clee would be helpless.

But on the fringe of the milling mêlée, a figure broke away, spurring downhill, fading from sight rapidly in the incredibly thick snowfall. Clee shouted — "Sergeant, take over!" — and raked his spurs viciously on the horse's sides. The animal sprang ahead, heedlessly took the steep and treacherous slope. At a dead run, Clee rode him, down the precipitous bank, to level ground.

The figure appeared briefly before him, sailing across an arroyo. Clee tried to lift his own animal across, but the horse saw the trap too late. He jumped, made the far bank on his forefeet, with his hind feet frantically clawing for purchase.

Clee was flung, limp and helpless, over the animal's head. He landed on his back, and the wind was driven out of him. He lay for but an instant, gasping, sucking desperately for air. With pain like a knife in his lungs, he rolled and came to his knees.

His horse, relieved of his weight, scrambled out of the arroyo and began to move away. Clee thought he could not get to his feet. But he forced himself up. Jeffords would not get away! By God, he would not!

Still clutching his soaked revolver, he ran for the horse, stumbling and sliding in the powdery snow. He caught the stirrup, and the animal began to trot. Clee cursed viciously, but then he caught a flying rein, and yanked the horse to a halt.

Immediately he was up again in the saddle. He circled back, picked up the tracks of Jeffords's horse, already dimming from the driving snow.

His spurs drew blood from the horse's steaming sides. The animal leaped ahead, and Clee's body whipped backward with the force of his leap. But he was running ahead, guiding the horse along the trail Jeffords had left.

How much time had he lost? A minute? Five? Either might mean the difference between success and failure. And it was growing darker. Jeffords's trail was increasingly difficult to follow. If Clee were forced to slow, or if he missed the trail, if only for an instant, then he would fail.

A burning, towering rage began to grow in him. His eyes were nearly blinded by the snow crusted on his brows and lashes. He blinked and, when he looked again, missed the trail. Not slowing, he drew the horse minutely to the left, then back again to the right. Ah! He had it now. Dimmer it was, growing fuzzier every minute. But he still had it. Perhaps his horse would put a foot into a prairie-dog hole.

The branch of a cedar whipped against his face, stung his eyes, blinded him. And when he looked again, the trail was gone. Again he tried this trick of pulling back and forth. But even that did not produce it.

What is the emotion that tears a man when he has a desperately wanted quarry in his hands and sees that quarry slip away? Rage is a mild term. Fury is puny beside it.

For a quarter hour he quested back and forth, searching. Once, he thought, he had found the trail, but so badly was it drifted over that he could never have followed it. Besides, he was aware that it could as easily be the trail of an antelope or deer as that of Jeffords.

At last he gave up, and rode to the left upward through the scattered cedars until he reached the road. Then he retraced his way along it until the bulk of the coach and the shifting shapes of troopers and prisoners loomed before him.

His face was white and still. Too many times had he been thus defeated, by first one thing and then another. He made himself a solemn promise there in the cold, chilling snow. He would hunt Eames Jeffords down, if it took all of his life. And he would kill him.

Chapter Sixteen

Lieutenant Champion was F Company's only casualty. The Rebels had nine killed and four wounded. The stage continued, under a five man escort, and the remainder of the troop, with the Confederate killed and wounded and the disarmed prisoners, retraced its way through the blinding snowstorm to Denver City. But the town's elation and gratitude to the troop was a short-lived thing, lasting only a few short days. At the first report of a raided hen house, it disappeared entirely.

Massey and both of his patrol detachments returned shortly after the stagecoach foray. Champion's death had left the company short of a lieutenant, and Massey prevailed upon Clee to take the post. His nomination by Massey was received with enthusiasm by all the troop, who had either observed him during the stagecoach battle, or had heard of it at second-hand.

Endlessly, in early December, bitter wind howled across the high plains, driving snow before it. Christmas approached, with nothing in prospect for the troop save for bread and beef and little enough of that. They had not been paid since enlisting, nor was there now much prospect that they would be paid. The glory of the stagecoach skirmish had dimmed, and daily routine became boring and deadly. Merchants in the town became increasingly reluctant to honor Governor Gilpin's drafts upon the U.S. Treasury.

It was small wonder, then, that the troop considered the town fair game and proceeded accordingly. Clashes with the town's police force, organized during the first part of December, were frequent, but rarely dangerous. Pigs and chickens disappeared from their pens and coops in town and later reappeared on the mess tables at the Antelope House. Calves, cows, and horses were kept under lock and key by the aroused townspeople.

F Company earned, and rightfully, the sobriquet "Massey's Raiders" and strove mightily, every day, to brighten their reputation. The lock of a saloon storeroom would be broken, and a barrel of whiskey disappear. On one occasion, four of the troop rolled and wrestled a forty gallon barrel down F street to the barracks, only to find upon opening it that they had stolen forty gallons of vinegar. Forthwith, they returned and remedied their error, taking this time a keg of fine Kentucky bourbon.

Nanette remained at the Fremont House as the winter wore away, although Clee saw little of her. And when he did occasionally encounter her, she was cold and distant and not at all encouraging. Clee, with strengthened hatred and determination, in his mind added her to Jeffords's long list of conquests.

Sam Massey, sensing that something was amiss between the two, nevertheless held his silence, for he was adequately occupied in managing his rebellious troop, in trying to prevent any open clashes with either townspeople or police. And whenever the weather was at all mild, he would take the troop out onto the plains and try to work off a part of their excess energy.

Clee continued to mend and to gain weight, until on January 10th he received orders to accompany Captain Massey and fifty men to Fort Wise, on the Arkansas River. Ill-clothed and ill-provisioned, they set out, experiencing *en route* some of the bitterest weather of the season. A number of the men suffered from frostbite during the miserable, seemingly endless, ten-day journey.

In spite of the wholesale plunder of the town of Denver during the winter, all of the men, Clee noticed, had thinned considerably since he had first met them in the fall on the Vasquez. They were nervous and restless, and often quarrelsome. Fights were frequent. Their plundering became an expression of their contempt for civilians who would raise troops to protect them and then refuse to support the troops out of niggardliness and penury. In all companies of the first regiment, save Massey's, desertions were all too common.

Fort Wise was situated on the north bank of the Arkansas River. Its buildings were of stone set with adobe mud. All buildings had flat, sod roofs and packed dirt floors. The center of the compound consisted of a flat, open drill ground, surrounded by quarters and stables forming a square. Colonel Bent's new fort was nearby, being situated on a rocky ridge that ran to the water's edge a short distance below.

In the quarters assigned to Massey's troop, there were neither furniture nor bedding, neither chairs, tables, nor eating utensils. Clothing, blankets, and arms were necessarily thrown onto the dirt floors. But somewhere, somehow, the men of the troop obtained hammers and saws, and in the early hours of the morning Clee and Sam Massey could hear the sounds of banging and sawing in the troop's quarters. Wagon boxes disappeared from the stables, and furniture magically appeared in the troop's quarters, and both Sam and Clee wholly ignored the process of transition. Sam reasoned that the government owed these men at least a bearable place to live, and, if they would not provide it directly, then let them provide it indirectly.

Determination and unscrupulousness were all that could have made the stay at Wise tolerable. When they considered the fare too plain, they openly robbed the sutler's store. And when searching regulars found proof of their guilt in F Company's quarters, Sam maneuvered it in such a way that an investigating board composed of himself and Clee repaid the sutler's loss out of their own pockets, and the matter was dropped.

The last of January, Sam was ordered back to

Denver for the remainder of his company. Dispatches had been received sporadically, indicating that General Sibley was preparing to march upon Fort Craig in southern New Mexico.

Sam left Clee in charge, cautioning wryly: "Try to keep them out of open war with the regulars, Clee. By God, they'd better give us some Rebels to fight, or they'll wish they had. I'd bet on my fifty against a full company of regulars any day."

With two troopers, he rode out, arriving in Denver in the evening a week later. He found that the troop had been removed from the Antelope House to Camp Weld, just south of town, with the object of ridding the town of their unwelcome attentions. He found as well that the removal had failed in its objective.

In the space of a few short weeks, matters had rapidly gone from bad to worse. The merchants of Denver, wearying of supplying food and clothing to the troop on drafts issued by the governor on the U.S. Treasury, had refused further issuance. The troop had, therefore, taken it wholly upon themselves to provide their supplies. Rations remained a relatively simple problem. Clothing was quite another. Clothing was not stored in unlocked or haphazardly constructed buildings.

The night of Sam Massey's arrival, twenty of the men had descended on a merchant's store in Denver and blatantly requisitioned what clothing they needed, supplying cheerfully detailed lists of what they took, but refusing their names. A sentry feeling, as he told Sam, that — "Them fellers meant to go out, anyhow." — failed to challenge them, and, since their leader was the orderly sergeant, they were reported present both at roll call and at tattoo.

The following morning, the merchant arrived at camp and complained to Colonel Slough. Perhaps because F Company had been the worst offender in the past, suspicion immediately fell there. Colonel Slough sent for the orderly sergeant and, after ascertaining that none of the company had been reported absent on the night in question, then said sardonically: "Sergeant, a man answering your description led the party that robbed this gentleman."

He turned to the merchant. "Is this the man?"

The merchant, a bald, stocky, middle-aged man, peered at the sergeant through thick-lensed glasses. "I think he is, sir."

The sergeant surged forward. "Hold on, you." He fished a set of brass knuckles from his pocket. "No lies about me, bucko, or I'll use these on you."

"Sergeant!"

The sergeant looked aggrieved. "Hell, sir, you think I should just stand here an' let 'im accuse me? Not me! No, sir!" He glared at the merchant, made a threatening gesture. Sam Massey hid a smile behind his hand. The sergeant said: "You lie about me, bucko, and I'll push them teeth of yours right down your fat throat!"

The merchant's eyes widened. "I didn't say it was you. I said the man looked like you."

Colonel Slough shrugged. "All right, Sergeant."

The sergeant went out, and Sam Massey followed unobtrusively. He caught the sergeant's arm as the man stepped out the door. He said, unsmiling: "You know, Sergeant, the city marshal will probably be down here before the day's over to search the barracks. It'd go hard with the man who was caught with that merchant's goods."

The sergeant stared at him, then began to grin. "It would at that, sir. It would at that. But you can count on F Company, sir."

Sam shrugged, said dryly: "I knew I could."

The merchant waddled out, angry and puzzled. Sam went back into the colonel's office. Slough frowned. "Why don't you keep those bastards in line, Sam?"

Sam said: "Listen, Colonel. They haven't been paid for five months. They haven't had a decent meal that wasn't stolen in all that time. The clothes they're wearing were bought with their own money. It's damned cold, and it'll be colder. I don't blame them a bit."

Slough shrugged regretfully. "Neither do I. I'll fill out a requisition so that merchant can get a draft from the governor for whatever that's worth."

Sam said: "I'm taking the rest of the troop

south to Wise as soon as I can get them ready. Then they'll be out of your hair." He grinned and went outside.

At noon, the city marshal showed up with the merchant. As Sam had suspected, the search unearthed nothing. But on the following morning, he could not help but notice how much more warmly dressed were some twenty men of the company.

Through a foot of snow, Sam Massey led the remainder of the troop, arriving at Fort Wise on February 20th. Almost immediately after that, an order was published, assigning the Colorado First Regiment to the support of Canby in New Mexico.

The order occasioned considerable satisfaction, as did the recurring reports of General Sibley's northern advance. At last, on March 1st, in early dusk, a messenger arrived from Fort Craig, reporting the engagement of Sibley's forces at Val Verde and the resulting defeat of the Union forces.

Sibley was on his way. Nothing stood between him and Colorado but Fort Union, poorly garrisoned with green, frightened troops. Marching orders were published immediately, and after a day and a half of preparation, on March 3, 1862, at noon, the command moved out.

Chapter Seventeen

On the first day out, the column encountered snow, driving down out of the north, thickening as night drew near. The foot soldiers slogged along patiently, miserably. Since F Company was mounted, it drew the scouting duty. Clee Fahr found this to his liking, since it gave him a chance to ride alone, a chance to try to sort his confused thoughts. He wished now that he had not been so stiff-backed the day he had left Denver. What would it have mattered, if Nan had been angry? He should have seen her, should have talked to her, should have told her good bye.

He had thought that the long months would dim the memory of Nan, would still the feeling of guilt that lay so heavily within him. He had thought he would be able to forget her. But he could not forget, and he did not want to forget. He admitted that he had let resentment — because of Eames Jeffords's attentions to her — color his own actions. He knew that, if it had not been for Jeffords, he would have gone to Nan, would have tried to iron out the misunderstanding that stood between them.

Now that it was too late, he reluctantly admitted that, even if Jeffords had been successful with Nan, it could make no difference in his love for her. For if Jeffords had had his way with her, no one was to blame but Clee. If Clee himself had made his offer of marriage to her out of the real feeling of love that stirred him, rather than out of a confused feeling of obligation . . . ?

New hatred for Jeffords burned in his thoughts. The man soiled everything he touched. And he had touched Clee, and Clee's women too often. He had spoiled Sibyl for Clee, and now, perhaps, he had spoiled Nan as well. Clee began to feel a wild anticipation for the action that impended somewhere in the south. If he could see Jeffords, if he could get the man in his sights. . . . He was certain that Jeffords was riding with Sibley. He could go nowhere else.

They encamped for the night less than a dozen miles from Fort Wise and, in the morning, continued westward along the Arkansas, making camp on the second night at Bent's old fort. There they were met by Captain Garrison, chief of subsistence at Fort Union, on his way to Fort Wise by stagecoach. From him, Clee heard the first account of the battle of Val Verde, of the crushing defeat the Union had suffered, of the utter collapse of discipline and resistance among the green, volunteer troops, of their cowardice and desertion.

Perhaps spurred by Garrison's real concern, Lieutenant Colonel Tappan, in command, ordered a forced march, allowing but a change of shirts and a couple of blankets to each man. The wagons and supplies were to follow behind as swiftly as possible.

Therefore, in the morning, they struck out across country, leaving the Arkansas and heading toward the Purgatoire, some seventy-five miles distant, and on the fourth day were re-united with the regiment at the crossing of the Purgatoire. With typical foresight, the regiment had provided a plenitude of supplies and trans-portation, these having been commandeered along the route of march. There were fully fifty wagons and perhaps two hundred horses, and supplies of whiskey and rations in temporary abundance.

In the morning they trailed out, nearly a thou-sand men in all. Steadily they climbed through-out the day into the cedared fastnesses of the Raton Mountains, glimpsing occasionally the tall, gleaming, white crests of the Spanish Peaks to westward. At noon of the following day, they reached the summit of Raton Pass, and began the precipitous descent into New Mexico.

Clee rode half a mile ahead of the column. It was perhaps two miles from the summit that he encountered the ambulance, creaking its slow and labored way toward the top. Clee rode up to it openly. Upon the driver's seat sat a bearded regular, chewing tobacco, cursing with monoto-nous and bored regularity at his tired mules. Seeing Clee, he drew them to a halt.

"Howdy."

Clee nodded, asked: "From Fort Union?"

The man spat, grunted. "Uhn-huh. Headin'

fer Fort Wise on the Arkansas."

"How are things at Union?"

The man squinted up at him warily. "D'pends on who wants to know."

Clee grinned. "I'm Lieutenant Fahr. First Colorado Volunteers. I'm riding scout. If you've got any information, I'll take you back to the colonel."

The regular relaxed, although his respect was grudging. "Lieutenant, things at Fort Union is pure hell. Less'n four hundred men in the garrison. Sibley on his way. The troops at Union are all green an' half scared to death. Communications is out 'tween Union an' Fort Craig. I reckon, if you fellers want to find Fort Union there, you'd better get a move on."

Clee heard the vanguard of the regiment approaching behind him. He whirled his horse and rode back to Colonel Slough. He said: "Colonel, there's an ambulance ahead that's heading north from Fort Union. You might want to question the driver. He says things are pretty bad."

The column halted, while Slough questioned the ambulance driver. When he had finished, his face was grave. He ordered the march resumed at an increased pace. At three o'clock, when the command reached the banks of Red River, he left all supplies behind in charge of a corporal's guard and, allowing nothing to the men but their arms and a couple of blankets apiece, resumed the way toward Fort Union, eighty miles away.

Afternoon faded into dusk and dusk into

night. Even with all the wagons loaded with men, there were still some four hundred who had to walk. A chill wind blew from the north. At eight, the colonel ordered a thirty-minute rest, and the men squatted listlessly and ate their cold rations. When the wagons were again loaded, it was with the men who had marched all afternoon.

Clee rode down the line in darkness, eyeing the horses, eyeing the men who slogged along, too tired to talk, too tired to do anything but put one foot ahead of the other, endlessly, repetitiously. The silence was broken only by the sounds of tramping feet, the rattle of wagons and harness.

Suddenly a man shouted. Brief confusion stirred the line ahead of Clee. A horse lay dead in harness, and his mate stood listlessly by, head hanging. Slough rode up beside Clee, yelling: "Get out and walk. Leave the wagon, and cut that horse loose."

And the column went on. More horses dropped in their harness. And more wagons were left behind, until they marked the trail, gaunted skeletons, each with a dead and freezing horse carcass beside it.

At three in the morning, Slough called a halt. Men dropped where they stood, simply wrapping themselves in their blankets and flinging themselves to the snowy ground.

Clee rubbed his horse down, well knowing that continued transportation depended on the animal's well-being, and staked him out to graze. Then he, too, rolled himself in his blankets and fell instantly asleep.

At first dawn, Sam Massey nudged him awake. Sam's face was drawn and haggard. Clee felt as if he had some monstrous hangover. He found his horse, saddled, and led the animal to the huge fire. He drank a cup of scalding coffee, wolfed a plate of beans.

He noticed that the men were eating hard bread with their coffee, and the beans seemed to form an unwelcome lump in his stomach. The bugle sounded, and, cursing and grumbling, the men got to their feet and straggled southward.

Sam's mounted company went out on scout, for there was a chance that Sibley had taken Union easily and had marched on past. As the morning progressed, the wind beat with increased strength out of the north. Snow and sleet whirled around the shivering, miserable men, mostly poorly clad. Their shoes were worn through, and occasionally Clee passed a man squatted in the blinding snow, wrapping a scarf or a shirt or a piece of a blanket about his feet.

Horses dropped and lay where they fell. Clee spent a good part of the day walking, leading his spent horse. Snow lay on his clothes, and wind sifted and drove through them. He wondered if he would ever be warm again.

A major's two fine grays and his saddle horse died, and the major walked. At noon, Clee saw Sam, squatted against a tree, and Sam asked him bitter. "What damned good will we be when we do get there? Sibley could cut us to pieces."

Clee shrugged, and the nightmare of marching went on. Wagons now carried only the sick of which there were plenty. And there were fewer wagons each mile they traveled. At Maxwell's Ranch, a halt was called, a beef butchered, and Maxwell generously provided the regiment with a hundred pounds of coffee, a hundred and sixty of sugar. With their bellies filled with coffee and half-raw meat, the men marched again.

Night found them at the Reyado, where Colonel Slough reluctantly concluded that to continue the march would be to invite serious consequences, and that arrival at Union with a spent regiment would be folly. Clee did not even bother to eat. He rolled himself in his blankets and slept.

The following day was much the same as those which had preceded it. It was, however, made more bearable by the sure knowledge that it would be the last of marching, at least for a while, the last of short rations and worn-out boots. Thirty miles remained to be traveled, and it took the exhausted regiment the entire day to cover it.

Long after dark they marched into Fort Union. Sam Massey and Clee, wasting no time, presented themselves at the quartermaster's storehouse almost before the troop had been dismissed. They drew all the rations and supplies they could think of, browbeating the alarmed regular in charge so mercilessly tha ୱୁe man was glad to see them go.

As there were no quarters immediately available for F Company, they built a fire in the corral with the horses, and crowded around it. The enlisted members of Sam's company had not been idle. Cases of champagne and wine, stolen from the sutler's storehouse, huge cheeses, and boxes of crackers littered the ground of the corral.

They were all oddly silent, as though from suppressed excitement. Clee, finding them short of blankets, took half a dozen men and went back to the quartermaster's storehouse. He drew a round hundred new blankets from the now thoroughly frightened clerk. When he got back, he found a keg of whiskey beside the fire, its top knocked in, and the men dipping into it with tin cups.

Sam Massey, grinning, lay in his blankets in a far corner of the corral. As Clee came up, he grumbled: "Hell, let 'em have whatever they can find tonight. We'll worry about talking our way out of it tomorrow."

It was with considerable surprise, and real pleasure, that Colonel Slough announced on the following morning: "It appears that, since I am senior officer present, I am in command of Fort Union. You will requisition your needs from the quartermaster. Clothing, arms, and rations are plentiful here, so ask for whatever you need."

Grown, hardened men were like so many boys raiding a pantry. Never had they seen such abundance of arms and clothing. When night fell, only one thing was missing, that being liquor, for which they had no money, and which the Army could not and would not issue. With typical unconcern they remedied the deficiency by a raid on the sutler's storehouse.

Daily now, Sam Massey and Clee drilled the troop for short periods each morning and again each afternoon. The horses rapidly gained strength on the double ration of grain they were getting. Rumors raged like grass fires through the post. Orders arrived from Colonel Canby, instructing Colonel Slough to remain at Fort Union and garrison the post. But the colonel had not accepted his commission to stagnate at Union for the duration of the war. He elected to ignore Canby's orders, and so, on March 22nd, the regiment marched out for Santa Fé, where it was rumored Sibley was presently staying.

Sergeant O'Rourke, with a detail of twenty men, left the fort early, loaded with plunder from the sutler's warehouse, which they buried at strategic locations along the line of march. A squad of regulars, sent after them, but having no inclination to tangle with Massey's miners, were careful to discover nothing and reported back shortly to the fort.

At roll call, about eleven, Sam Massey discovered that some forty of the company were missing. He turned to Clee. "Ride over to the Lome. Roust them out of there and bring them along." The Lome was a small settlement, some five miles from Fort Union, where the needs of the troop which could not be supplied at the post were adequately satisfied by a dozen Mexican prostitutes.

It took Clee three hours to gather the missing men, sober them up, and get them into their saddles. He rode into camp at dusk, ten miles from Fort Union, the stragglers forming a ragged group before him.

Clee was beginning to feel some doubt as to what the efficacy of these troops would be, pitted against Sibley's trained and seasoned irregulars. He was beginning to wonder if, outnumbered three to one by Sibley, they would even be able to make a show against such a superior force. Sam seemed to have no such doubts, seemed to feel little concern over the troops' drunk and disorderly conduct.

The following morning they continued southward, camping in the evening at Las Vegas, a small Mexican settlement. Again the troopers of Massey's F Company got completely out of hand, drinking and carousing with the Mexican women of the town until the wee hours of morning.

On the Twenty-Fourth the entire command continued to Bernal Springs where they encamped, but Massey's company was ordered on another eight miles to rendezvous with three other companies of cavalry, numbering about one hundred and fifty men, and on the Twenty-Fifth, infantry, numbering one hundred and eighty men, arrived from Bernal Springs under command of Major Chivington, traveling in wagons.

Tension continued to build up in all the men. It was rumored that they were to make a swift dash on Santa Fé, and it seemed certain that they were to see action at long last. With two days' rations in their saddlebags, the force moved out, camping that night at Koslowski's ranch near the mouth of Apache Cañon. A twenty-man scouting force under Lieutenant Nelson came in that night with four of Sibley's pickets, captured at Pigeon's Ranch, some five miles distant. From them it was ascertained that a force of Rebels was advancing through La Glorieta Pass. Now, with action a certainty, the troop suddenly stopped grumbling and carousing and became silently and grimly earnest.

At eight in the morning, the force, numbering some four hundred men, moved out, with the infantry leading, the cavalry bringing up the rear. Sam's company was broken up, a part of it being used to scout, the remainder riding in the rear with the other three companies of cavalry.

Clee rode out in front with a force of thirty men. All through the morning they poked along, pacing their rate of march to the slower speed of the infantry behind. Near noon they passed through Pigeon's Ranch, where the pickets had been captured the day preceding, and then continued their advance into Apache Cañon.

At two, Clee, riding in the lead, topped the

summit of the pass, and halted. A sudden, in-comprehensible excitement possessed him. His troopers bunched around him and O'Rourke asked: "See somethin', sir?"

Clee shook his head. He nudged his horse and moved downcountry. But he could not rid him-self of the oddly uneasy feeling that lingered in the back of his mind. Ahead, in the brushy bottom of the gulch, the road turned sharply.

From ahead, a horse nickered. Clee began to grin, but the grin died as he thought: *What if it's not a scouting force? What if it's the main body?*

But it was too late to worry about that. A gray-clad cavalryman came into sight, another, and another. The lead trooper was turned in his saddle, talking to the man behind him. Clee stood in his stirrups and yelled: "Now! Get after 'em!"

With a howl that seemed to spring simulta-neously from thirty throats, the troops behind and to both sides of him spurred forward. In a matter of minutes they had the Rebel scout de-tail surrounded and disarmed. Not a shot had been fired.

Clee questioned the lieutenant in charge swiftly. "How many men behind you? How far back are they? Where's your main force?"

The lieutenant shook his head. "Go to hell."

Clee shrugged, turning to O'Rourke: "Take 'em back." Then he deployed his remaining troopers to both sides of the road to wait for Chivington and the main force to come up.

Chapter Eighteen

The sun beat down warmly upon Clee's shoulder blades. Cautioning his men to stay under cover, he rode upslope, concealed by junipers, and from a high point viewed the wide, flat valley. He saw the vanguard of Rebel troops come into sight at a bend of the cañon, hearing behind him the ragged noises made by Chivington's force, advancing from the opposite direction.

Brief concern touched him as he wondered if Chivington were close enough. At that instant, the Confederate forces saw Chivington's command before them, and halted in utter, bewildered surprise. But they recovered quickly. A bugle blared its brassy notes across the field. The Confederates unfurled their red flag, the lone-star banner of Texas, and, with it waving, came forward at a trot. Clee tried to find Jeffords among the gray-clad troops, ceased this almost instantly with a sense of the futility of it.

On the far side of the valley, the road crossed a deep arroyo over a plank bridge, and, as the Confederates streamed over this bridge, it rang hollowly in the clear air. With precision and utter lack of confusion, the Rebel artillery — two howitzers — moved up and emplaced in the center of the wide valley. Mounted infantry curvetted briefly about the artillery pieces but, when they were ready to fire, retired immediately to the rear. Clee reined his horse around, saw Chivington's infantry bunching in confusion. He thought: *My God! That grape will cut them to pieces!*

There was an unreality to this scene, but it ended with the roar of the howitzers. Grape and canister screamed into the ranks of Chivington's troops. Horses reared and screamed, fell threshing to the ground. Men yelled hoarsely. In that moment, a rout seemed certain. But Chivington's bull bellow rolled across the field, audible for more than a half mile, rallying, scattering his terrified men.

"Massey! Howland! Get your cavalry to the rear! Charge that artillery, if they start to retreat! Wyncoop! Anthony! Skirmishers into that timber on the slope! Downing! Up the other slope! Keep under cover, but damn it, pour it on!"

The command hesitated. The howitzers roared again, and again the grapeshot rained amongst them.

Clee could hear the conflicting shouts of the captains of the infantry companies. Order emerged slowly, almost reluctantly, out of the chaos. The bunched Coloradoans split, a part of them rushing up the slope to the right, others to the left. The cavalry galloped to the rear.

Clee turned for one more reluctant look at the enemy. He was directly between them and

Chivington's force, but he had been ordered to the rear to await signs of retreat on the part of the Confederates. He briefly wondered if his thirty men could charge and take the two murderous howitzers. He looked at Chivington, a towering, huge figure in full regimentals, fearlessly sitting his horse in plain view of both enemy riflemen and artillery. Clee could see the spurs of dust kicked up around the major by the rain of bullets.

He felt a quick and boundless admiration for the man and, admitting that Chivington's plan of battle was sound, gave no further consideration to disregarding the major's orders. Raising a hand, he spurred his horse back through the trees, and his command fell in reluctantly behind. Hardly had they gone a hundred yards before they passed Wyncoop's and Anthony's skirmishers, advancing along the slope through the timber. These men worked along the timber's fringe, dropping off one by one to squat and pour their murderous fire into the Confederates below.

Clee felt a rising, continuous satisfaction. Thus easily could an imminent rout be turned to advantage by a determined and fearless commander. Clee had never particularly liked Chivington, who was a Baptist minister turned soldier, a pious martinet, whose desire to turn the First into a spit and polish outfit had earned him only dislike. Yet there was no denying the man's ability, or his pure, raw courage. Clee doubted suddenly if another man in the outfit could have handled this action as well.

Flanked, with rifle fire pouring into them from both sides, the Rebels, who plainly outnumbered the Coloradoans by more than two hundred, began to show signs of retreat. Clee momentarily lost sight of the battle as he thundered downslope out of the timber and at full gallop, with his men behind, rode to join Massey and Howland at the rear.

Massey was fidgeting, glowering, straining at the bit. "God damn it!" he roared at Howland. "Let's move up . . . let's get up there!"

Howland shook his head. He was a regular officer, one of Fort Union's complement, and his expression made no attempt to conceal his disapproval of Massey and his undisciplined regulars. He said: "Chivington's strategy is sound. The function of cavalry is not to waste themselves in a suicidal assault on artillery."

Massey groaned. Clee turned his horse, watched the progress of the battle. He could see the infiltrating forms of the infantry on both slopes, working their inexorable way forward, until they formed an irregular crescent about the Rebels on the valley floor.

Behind the Rebels was the arroyo, too deep to be used as a rifle pit, spanned by the single narrow bridge. The Rebels began to fall back, crossing the bridge in groups of thirty or forty. The artillery suddenly began to move.

Massey howled: "Come on!"

Howland's voice was curt and sharp. "Captain! God damn it, I'll remind you that I'm in command here. We'll move, when I give the order."

"But they're retreating. Damn you, they'll get clear away."

Indecision was briefly mirrored in Howland's face. Then the moment for attack was gone. With a rumble, plainly audible even at this distance, the artillery crossed the bridge.

Demolition squads dropped into the arroyo beneath it. Clee could not conceal his disgust, nor could Sam Massey conceal his. With decisive victory in their grasp, it had been suddenly lost by Howland's indecision and disregard of orders.

The demolition squads scurried up out of the arroyo, ran frantically toward the rear. The bridge seemed to lift into the air, and then, as black-powder smoke billowed up around it, disintegrated, and fell out of sight into the arroyo. The explosion made a dull thud at this distance, and the ground trembled slightly. Back down in the valley the Rebels went, and they replaced the howitzers behind the arroyo this time, safe from cavalry attack.

Chivington's roar placed instant blame for Howland's disregard of orders: "Howland! Dismount your men! Join the infantry here!"

Howland gave the order to his men. "Dismount. Horse holders to the rear."

Then Chivington again: "Massey! Charge at my signal!"

Massey began to smile. He moved up, his men following, until they were but three hundred yards from the yawning brink of the arroyo. Sam turned to Clee. "How wide is that ravine?"

Clee shrugged. "There at the bridge . . . maybe ten, twelve feet."

"Can a horse jump it?"

"The Rebs don't think so. That's why they destroyed the bridge."

"I do think so. I think we can jump across." Sam's jaw was hard, his eyes narrowed. "Chivington thinks we can, too."

Regrouped behind the yawning arroyo, the Rebels made a new stand. Their howitzers raked the hillsides, poured deadly fire into Chivington's troops on the valley floor. But Wyncoop and Anthony on the one side, Downing on the other, continued to advance along the hillside, again flanking the Rebs, again enveloping them in a murderous crossfire.

Behind him now, on the field of battle, Clee could see the struggling forms of horses, of wounded men. A shrill scream lifted as grapeshot took one of Chivington's men in the belly. A man directly beside Clee put a hand to his bloody throat, choked, and tumbled from his saddle.

Impatience and rage began to mount in Clee. Always his eyes quested across the field, futilely searching for Eames Jeffords's slight, wiry figure. What would he do if he saw Jeffords? He shrugged. There would be nothing he could do.

At least until Sam Massey gave the order to charge.

Rebel skirmishers had climbed to a high, rocky point commanding the former bridge site, prepared apparently to pour a concentrated fire downward upon Chivington's men if they attempted to cross the arroyo at this, its narrowed point.

But Downing's men scrambled up the mountain like goats, eventually placing themselves above the Rebels and then, from the shelter of rocks and brush clumps, poured down their deadly and withering fire. On the far side of the cañon, Wyncoop and Anthony followed Downing's example, and soon were above the Confederate forces on that side as well.

For more than an hour the battle continued in this way, while men fell and crawled away, while they died moaning or in silence in the bright sunlight. At last, the Rebels abandoned their rocky point, and with a rush descended onto the valley floor. Behind they left the gray-clad bodies of their dead.

Chivington raised an arm, yelled the single word: "Massey!"

Massey drew his saber. Waving it above his head, he shouted — "All right! Over the gulch! Charge!" — and he swept into motion with a vicious dig of his spurs.

Involuntarily Clee's heels dug into his own mount's sides. Behind him, a long, high yell lifted, coming from a hundred throats at once.

Again it was like the first night he had seen these men, brawling across the clearing at Idaho, only this time it was real.

The company swept forward, gaining speed. The brink of the arroyo loomed ahead, and for an instant Clee wondered if the horses could reach that far. Grimly he thought: *They'll jump, or they'll die in a pile at the bottom!*

As though suddenly realizing that in their utter, suicidal recklessness this troop of cavalry intended to jump the arroyo, the Confederates concentrated every ounce of their firepower on the charging riders. A horse racing beside Clee went on its knees, throwing its rider, then somersaulting. Clee reined aside savagely, escaping the threshing hoofs of the downed animal by a margin of inches.

Massey sailed across, light in his saddle. Clee's own horse came to the brink, and Clee lifted him lightly across. He landed, running, clearing the far side with his hind feet by such a small margin that he kicked loose dirt into the arroyo.

Breathlessly, Clee glanced behind. Never, he knew, would he see another sight like this. Standing in their stirrups, leaning forward, their eyes alight with the joy and recklessness of the savage moment, the troop came over behind him. One horse missed by a full three feet and disappeared into the arroyo in a cloud of dust, its rider's face white and filled with terror.

Full in their faces the cannons roared. But elevated as they were for longer range, the grape whistled overhead. And before they could depress the muzzles of the howitzers, F Company was upon them, sharp hoofs killing as effectively as swords and pistols.

The Rebels broke, lost all restraint, and sought to flee. But there is no flight afoot from mounted men. Massey's raiders rode them down, splitting them with sabers, shooting them with revolvers. Clee swept on past the howitzers, down the valley. The troop spread out, so as to cover the routed Confederates. They overtook them, killed, and swept on past.

Massey, huge in his saddle, waving his dripping saber, turned them, and again they charged back through the utterly disorganized enemy. The valley was a mass of fleeing, gray-clad troops. A glance upward at the slope showed Clee both Anthony and Wyncoop, racing with their companies over the rough ground of the slope. They seemed to be attempting the same maneuver.

Sam, riding along beside Clee, grunted heavily, and slapped a huge hand at his thigh. It came up bloody, and Sam stared at it stupidly for a moment. In the roar of confusion, of shots and shouts, it was impossible to distinguish any single report. Yet, as Clee looked ahead, he saw a bearded, hatless Reb squatted on the ground, sighting his rifle again at Sam.

He reined swiftly over, and rode directly at the gray-clad marksman. His revolver lifted, bucked in his hand. As though driven aside by a rough push, the Reb tumbled to the ground, rolling and coming quickly to his knees. Clee's gun spat at him again, and this time, when he hit the ground, he remained still.

A bullet grazed Clee's cheek, stinging and bringing blood. He saw a vaguely familiar face over his sights, and withheld pressure on the trigger. He swept on past, leaving the man alive behind him. He half heard the shout — "Clee!" — while his brain rummaged through the past, seeking the man's name. This was the hell of it, a nation fighting internally, friend against friend, brother against brother. Whoever that was back there had known Clee, and Clee had known him.

Every gray-clad officer caught his eye, held his glance briefly. Like an ebbing tide, the gray wave of retreat rolled back down the wide valley. Where the cañon narrowed at the far end, Wyncoop and Anthony on the one side, Downing on the other, closed in with their men like pincers. Chivington pressed from the rear, and the cavalry, under wounded Sam Massey, harassed the straggling survivors.

Prisoners in small groups were constantly passing now. Sam had halted his company, halted to regroup and to give the horses a blow. Clee saw the man again, the man whom he had spared and who had called his name. He rode over, walking his horse beside the man, looking down. He said: "I know you, but damned if I can recall your name."

The man was short, his thick legs inclined to

bow. His hair was gray, his face clean-shaven. His eyes were a humorous blue. He grinned. Blood smeared one side of his face, welling from a scalp wound. He said: "Juergens, suh. I was ove'seah fo' youah uncle in Geo'gia." His smile was unutterably weary, and Clee suddenly felt the weariness in himself that nearly three hours of battle and tension can cause.

Clee asked sharply: "You remember Eames Jeffords, then?"

"I do that, suh."

"Where is he?"

The man gestured shortly with his head. "Back theah. He wasn't with us today."

Clee said: "The war's over for you now. Good luck."

"Thanks, suh." And Juergens bent his head and went on.

Unnoticed, the sun had dipped below the mountains to westward. Now, a chill fell over the battleground. Stretcher-bearers plodded back toward Pigeon's Ranch. The dead stared at the darkening sky, unseeing. Clee began to shiver.

He joined Sam at the head of the company. Chivington rode up to them, ordering shortly: "Act as rear guard. It's too late to chase them now." There was a fierce glow in Chivington's uncompromising, hard stare. As he rode away, he called back, "A good job. A damned good job."

Clee ordered the troop to dismount. He had half the horses unsaddled and rubbed down.

When that was finished, the other half. Then he posted guards and let the men slump to the ground and rest.

Night sifted from the heavens, blotting out the ugliness and horror of the battlefield, dimming its sights and its smells. The noise of the victorious Coloradoans faded as the last of the stragglers filed past.

A trooper said: "The poor bastards didn't have a chance after we jumped that arroyo. And they're just like us. I killed a kid that couldn't've been over sixteen."

A harsh voice interrupted: "Shut up! For Christ's sake, shut up!"

Another said: "Yeah. Shut up!"

Clee wished for a cigar. He shivered, and he thought of Nanette. His mind was drugged with exhaustion. It seemed no longer to matter to him what had passed between her and Jeffords. He could only remember the way she had been in his arms.

Hours later, a rider came from Chivington, ordering them in. Today had been a victory, but it was not yet over. They had met but a small portion of Sibley's troops. Tomorrow, they would meet the rest.

Chapter Nineteen

The following day was not a day of battle, however. Chivington and Major Pyron, the Confederate commander, arranged a truce to allow the day for burial of their dead and care of the wounded. Wagons went out to the battlefield, and, when they came back, they were loaded with the Colorado dead. In the buildings at Pigeon's, the surgeons and their assistants worked throughout the day with the wounded. Occasionally, all day long, from these buildings issued screams and long, pain-filled shouts.

A detachment of mounted infantry was sent with the Rebel prisoners, numbering nearly eighty, to escort them to Fort Union. Sam Massey, with a ball in his thigh, was invalided out, much to his disgust.

During the night, some three hundred infantry and cavalrymen had moved up to Pigeon's from Bernal Springs where Slough was holding his reserves. But Chivington, finding the water supply at Pigeon's inadequate, ordered the regiment to fall back to Koslowski's, where the spring was large and pure.

In the afternoon of March 27th, the remainder of Slough's command moved up from Bernal Springs to Koslowski's, and at dawn of the following morning, anticipating that this day would see the decisive battle, Slough sent two columns toward Pigeon's for a reconnaissance in force.

He ordered about four hundred men, infantry and cavalry, under Major Chivington, over the rugged mountains to the south of La Glorieta Pass to scout the Confederates' rear, and harass it as opportunity presented. Clee rode with this group at the head of F Company, among whom there was considerable grumbling at the assignment they had been given.

Sam Massey sat before the main building at Pigeon's, whittling out a homemade crutch as the two columns from Koslowski's converged upon Pigeon's. The cavalry, which did not include Sam's F Company, came in first about eight-thirty, followed over the next hour and a half by the infantry, and finally by the wagon train, numbering over one hundred wagons.

They paused at Pigeon's to rest, built fires, stacked their arms. Most of those who had come up from Bernal Springs yesterday lay down on the ground to sleep. Those who had been in the battle of Apache Cañon, two days previously, clustered around the buildings, visiting the wounded. Sam thought, watching them: *Damn it, if I could get a horse . . . !*

He knew he could do no good trying to walk. He knew that Slough would not allow him with the cavalry. Yet he hated to miss the battle that he knew would occur today. Apache Cañon had been but a skirmish. The battle today would decide whether the Rebs marched north to Denver, or whether they retired to Texas, whence they had come.

He heard Slough bawling a command at the cavalry commander: "Send a detachment into the pass, with pickets out ahead! I want to know where those damned Texans are!"

Sam got up and tried his crutch. He grimaced at the pain that shot through his leg. But the crutch would do. He hobbled across the bare and dusty yard. At the well, men were clustered three deep, filling their canteens, for there would be no more water until they reached Cañoncito at the far end of La Glorieta Pass.

Suddenly a rider pounded toward them from the direction the cavalry had taken. He was standing in his stirrups, waving his hat, shouting: "Colonel! Colonel! The Rebs are here, less'n half a mile away from you!"

Slough ran toward him, yelling quick, brief orders. The bugles sang their brassy "Assembly." Sam Massey began to grin. It began to look as if he would see the fight in spite of his wound.

In confusion and fright, the Coloradoans scrambled for their stacked arms, tried to form some kind of order from the complete disorder. The Rebel artillery boomed out, loud and close, and heavy grapeshot crashed through the cottonwoods that clustered about the buildings at Pigeon's. A round shot tore into the main house, taking out a section of adobe wall. Explosive shells burst among the confused Coloradoans.

Sam could see the smoke of the artillery, rising

from the point of a ridge half a mile to westward, from another point across a deep and narrow gulch from the first. He could see the glint of sunlight upon the Confederates' arms and equipment, and knew at once that they were emplaced in a horseshoe formation on both these high ridges and behind them, facing the narrow gulch. He could see Captain Chapin's company of cavalry, dismounted, climbing through the timber toward the securely emplaced Confederates. Rifle fire broke out on the ridge. He saw men collapsing up there, limp and lifeless.

Infantry broke away from the ranch, trotting at the double, to approach the foot of the ridge across the long, bare space that lay before the ranch. Grapeshot rained among them. They broke ranks, and spread out.

Sam saw Captain Ritter's battery of artillery, supported by Captain Sopris's company of infantry, rumble across the open valley toward the north, saw them emplace on the road at its upper end. Lieutenant Claflin's battery, supported by Captain Robbins's company, toiled upward through the timber to emplace along the trees high on the point of the ridge.

Sam got up, went inside, and strapped on his revolver. He found a rifle, forgotten in the excitement, on the ground outside. The surgeon yelled at him, but Sam did not turn. Hobbling, using the rifle as a crutch now, he crossed the valley, and bellied down behind a rock at the foot of the ridge. The roar of the cannon, above and to his right was deafening. Shot made a whistling sound as it passed over his head.

A gray-clad Rebel scrambled across a clearing near the top of the ridge. Sam leveled his rifle, fired, and the man pitched forward on his face. Fierce, crackling rifle fire broke out along his left. The roar of artillery was continuous.

For two hours, Sam lay behind his rock, sniping upward at the Rebels high on the ridge, sniping with deadly accuracy. The Union artillery fell back, and emplaced again. The Union troops backed down the hill. Captain Downing's company, having advanced too bravely perhaps, found that they were engaging almost the entire Confederate force. Instead of retreating, they fought bravely, losing in killed and wounded a full half of their numbers before they were reinforced.

At noon, Slough ordered a general withdrawal, to new lines previously selected. The artillery, covered by rapid infantry fire, reëmplaced at the new positions and opened fire.

Still the battle raged at a thousand different points. Massey, hobbling along on his makeshift crutch, found himself a new position in a small irrigation ditch, and from there again opened fire upon the advancing Confederates. A man tumbled into the ditch with him, panting. Blood streamed from a raw gash in the man's head. He gasped: "I was out fer damned near an hour, I guess. When I come to, them damned Rebs was all around me. I crawled till I got through 'em, and then I ran. Jesus, man, this is awful." He stuck his head up to peer at the advancing gray lines.

Off to one side, Sam could hear the close and thunderous roar of Union artillery. All of the Confederate fire seemed to concentrate on this one spot. Sam yanked the man's leg, and pulled him down. "Keep your head down, if you don't want it blowed off. You picked a hell of a poor spot to catch your breath. The artillery ain't more'n fifty feet off to the right of us, an the Rebs aim to take it."

The effect of the Union grapeshot in the Confederate ranks was appalling. Men fell as though mowed down by some gigantic scythe. But more came over their prone bodies, and the gray line wavered across the valley, moving even closer. Their bayonets gleamed in the bright sunlight.

The man beside Sam pulled a stub of a cigar from his pocket and clamped it between his yellowed teeth. He said: "Damned if I know whether I'd rather chew this damned thing or smoke it."

Sam grinned, aimed, and squeezed his trigger. A Rebel pitched forward and lay still. Sam fired again. The man beside Sam grunted: "I heerd Slough talkin' to one of the officers. He said we was outnumbered more'n two to one. You reckon we'll get out of this alive?"

Sam shrugged. "Some will an' some won't. I guess there ain't a hell of a lot of use worryin' about it."

215

The Confederate lines were now less than a hundred yards away. The artillery commander must have double-shotted his guns, for their roar became deeper, more powerful. Sam saw a whole section of the Rebel line literally blown away, their shattered bodies forced back six or seven feet by the impact of small shot. Behind them, men arose from the ground, leaped over their bodies, and filled the gap in the line. Sam's gun was hot. The man beside him loaded and fired with steady regularity, cursing in a low voice all the while.

Sam wondered briefly how his company was faring. He thought about Nanette, and about Clee. He knew that in some way their own desire had come between them. He remembered the long, bitter, winter months, the endless waiting, all of it pointing at this seemingly endless, but all too brief, action. Finding himself this close to the Union artillery which was obviously the Confederates' present objective, he had, several minutes before, realized that in all probability he would not survive this action. He wished he could have talked to Clee, wished he could have asked him to look out for Nanette. Then he thought with quick certainty: *Why, I don't have to ask him that. He'll do it, anyway.*

The gray line was now at almost point-blank range. They were less than fifty yards away. Suddenly, above the din of battle, a roar sounded: "Fix your bayonets! Charge!"

Behind the guns, the supporting infantry rose

up, bayonets fixed to the long barrels of their guns. Blue clad, they swarmed past the guns, now silenced, to meet the oncoming gray-clad Rebels.

Sam felt like a coward because he could not walk. The man beside him got up hesitantly, but, as men came up from the rear and passed him, his hesitation vanished, and he began to move forward, trotting. Sam called: "So long, friend."

Now the blue line was between Sam and the Rebels. Sam got to his feet, using the rifle as a crutch, and hobbled forward, holding the revolver in his free hand. He thumbed back the hammer, aimed at a slouch-hatted figure twenty yards away, and pulled the trigger. He was behind his blue-clad comrades, but a few of the Rebels got through by the sheer force of their charge, and Sam fired at these until his gun was empty.

A bearded Rebel, waving an empty rifle by its barrel, came at him with a rush. Sam lifted his own rifle, parried the blow, then flung his empty revolver full in the man's face. Weakness clutched at him, weakness from his wound now aggravated by a day of excitement and action. He toppled, and brought his rifle down to keep himself from falling.

Something slammed against his shoulder, and immediately he found himself on his face on the ground. The tide of battle had moved over him and above him. A Confederate officer fell dead across his legs. A man stepped on his hand, but Sam, while conscious of it, neither seemed to have the strength to withdraw it, nor did he feel any pain. For a few moments the shouts and shots dimmed, and then again men rushed over him. Then, after what seemed an interminable length of time, the concussion of the artillery began to beat at his ears. He was out in front of them slightly now, and their concussion tore and whipped at his clothing each time they fired.

Sam smiled. So the attack had failed. A wet warmth seemed to be soaking Sam's shoulder. He stirred and, after a determined effort that lasted a full five minutes, managed to touch the shoulder with his other hand. He winced. His hand came away soaked with blood. Swiveling his head, he could see men bustling about in the open around the guns, bringing up their teams, preparing to move back. Panic clutched at Sam for the first time today. Now, he could not bear the thought of being left behind, of being captured or killed while he lay helpless on the ground.

He summoned all of his iron will and, lying on his unwounded side, reached with his unhurt arm, reached out ahead of him and began to crawl crabwise on the ground. The men in the ditch before him got to their feet and began to run toward the rear, and the howitzers rumbled into motion. Sam shouted. A couple of men looked back at him for a moment, hesitated, and finally returned. They hoisted him up between them and half carried him with them toward the rear. Pain became so intense in Sam's shoulder that he almost fainted. Sweat poured off his forehead, stinging his eyes, and his face was pasty gray.

Scattered rifle fire crackled from the new positions before them. Although he did not want to say them, Sam got out the words: "Hell, boys, I can crawl, I reckon. You go on before you git it in the back."

For a while neither said anything, and there were just the sounds of their panting and labored breath. Finally one of them muttered: "Well, I guess not. I guess, if we're goin' to git it, we'll git it no matter where we are."

Someone came up with a stretcher then, and they rolled Sam onto it. Consciousness faded and returned. He asked the man who plodded along above him: "Are we winnin' or losin'?"

"We ain't winnin'. That's the fourth time we've fallen back."

"Where the hell's the cavalry?"

He thought bitterness sounded in the man's voice. "Back at the rear with the supper train. They ain't fired a shot all day. They ain't intendin' to."

"Where's F Company? They git back yet?"

"No, by God. If they was here, we'd have some cavalry support!"

"What time is it?"

"Five o'clock."

Sam lost consciousness then. When he came to, he was in a wagon. The jolting, painful movement had awakened him. Up on the driver's seat, he could hear the murmured voices of two men. He wondered if they were the same ones who had carried him off the field. Outside, he could hear the harsh shouts of other teamsters, the jangle of harness and the endless creak of wheels, the shriek of iron tires against the rocks in the road.

The man on the seat said: "God damn it, talk about luck. Slough was gone an' so was 'most everyone else. All that was left there was Ritter's battery, an' they was loadin' an' firin', just like they'd been doin' all day. Cap'n Downing rode by on a hoss, an' Ritter looks up. He was goddamn' mad about Slough pullin' out. He says . . . 'Downing, you're the only officer left on the field. What are your orders to me?' Downing looks at him for a minute. Finally he says . . . 'Doubleshot your guns an' keep on firin'.' It wasn't more'n a minute after that when a Reb ambulance wagon comes chargin' up with a white flag whippin' from the top. It pulls up in front of Downing, an' a Reb officer gets out and asks for a truce till tomorrow noon. Hell, mebbe the Rebs didn't know Slough was quittin'."

"What happened?"

The other laughed. "I reckon Downing took his mad out on that Reb officer. He yanked him out of the ambulance an' tied his hands behind him. Then he blindfolds him. Then he shoved him back into the ambulance an' climbs in with him. The last I heard was him hollerin' at the driver, tellin' him which road to take to git him to

Koslowski's ranch."

There was a long silence. Sam grew drowsy in spite of the jolting discomfort of the wagon. As from a great distance, he heard the words: "I was in the infantry, supportin' Ritter's artillery. Right after Downing pulled out, Ritter gets up on one of the guns and yells . . . 'Boys, we jist cain't fight this war all by ourselves. Move out!' We didn't waste no time doin' what he said. About then you came up with your stretcher, an' we loaded it on this wagon. Keerist, I'm hungry!"

Sam scowled with bewilderment. There was no sense in what he had just heard. The Rebels were not fools. They could not have missed the fact that Slough was retiring from the field. Why, then, the truce? Why not a dawn march to Koslowski's and annihilation for the Coloradoans? Was this some treachery on the part of the Rebels? Sam knew he should stay awake, should warn Slough against this possibility of treachery. If Slough granted the truce, he would not be looking for a dawn attack. But the drain on his strength of this long day and the new wound and its attendant loss of blood were too great. Sam, in spite of his iron will and determination, lost consciousness.

Chapter Twenty

Clee rode that morning at the head of F Company, among whom there was considerable grumbling at the assignment they had been given. They had acquired a boundless confidence in Chivington, who had demonstrated two days before that he had not only courage but a tactical genius as well. Yet there was that in F Company which made them want to share in the decisive contest they knew was shaping up at Pigeon's Ranch for today.

Chivington himself seemed dissatisfied at the assignment which had been given him. No professional soldier, Chivington was nevertheless devoted to book soldiering, and looked with grim disapproval upon Slough's contention that the function of the Coloradoans was that of guerrillas. Yet, since Slough was in command, he had no choice but to obey.

In early morning, they marched past the ruins of the old Pecos Pueblo and, about a mile farther west, left the road to take a train that wound upward through San Cristóbal Cañon toward Galisteo. It was after ten, when Clee heard the booming of cannon behind him. He rode to Major Chivington. The tempo of artillery increased until it was like the distant roll of drums.

Chivington cursed and said wryly: "Well,

we're missing that. Take your company and scout back along the rim of La Glorieta Pass. I want to know what's behind me, when I jump their camp at Cañoncito."

Clee saluted. With his company, he peeled off and climbed the steep and thinly timbered ridge that paralleled the trail to northward. The boom of the cannon was incessant. Impatience stirred Clee. Back there a battle was in progress, a terrific battle from the sounds of artillery. And here he was, away from it, making a useless and fruitless scout through bare and uninhabited hills. Too, he was missing his chance at Jeffords. Or so he thought. Guarding carefully the strength of the horses, the company crossed a series of ridges, coming at last to a point, near noon, from which they could view the defile of La Glorieta Pass.

Here, Clee turned west, keeping the troop out of sight below the ridge line, yet always having flankers out on foot to slip from point to point along the rim and report the movement of the Confederates in the valley below. A mounted messenger thundered along the old Santa Fé Trail that wound its erratic way through the pass. An occasional ambulance rumbled audibly along toward the west, loaded presumably with the wounded. Once, a detachment of soldiers rode east from the westward end of the defile, over a hundred strong, and Clee thought: *Reinforcements of the Rebs at Pigeon's Ranch. That's about a hundred we won't have to fight today.*

The guns at Pigeon's grew fainter, but did not diminish the regularity of their firing as Clee and the troop continued to pile up the distance between themselves and the battle. The sun rose to its zenith in the sky and began its downward passage toward the western horizon. Near two o'clock, the company reached a point at last where they could look down into the Confederate camp below them. Clee dismounted, and bellied down atop a high point to watch. O'Rourke crawled up behind him.

"How many men you make out there, sir?" he asked.

"I've been trying to count. It doesn't look like there are too many. Two, three hundred, maybe."

"And damned near eighty wagons!" O'Rourke's voice was alive with excitement. "I'll bet you that's their whole damned supply train."

"If it is, we're lucky." But Clee shook his head, considering this. "Where's their horses?"

"I don't know." O'Rourke was worried suddenly. "You reckon this is a trap, Lieutenant?"

"I don't know, but I'll bet we can find out." He grinned at the burly sergeant. "You still sorry about this assignment?"

"No. Not any more." O'Rourke's chapped lips split into a wide grin. He crawled back toward the troop.

Clee withdrew his attention from the camp and stared about him at the tall, forbidding mountaintops. Suddenly he saw a glint of metal in the sunlight atop a high mountain a quarter

224

mile away. Between his own vantage point and this higher mountain lay a deep and rock-strewn gorge. He thought — *There's Chivington.* — and he wriggled back until he could get to his feet without being seen from below. He found his troop in the timber, and detailed a man to cross the gorge and report to Chivington for orders. Then Clee returned to the peak to study the land below him, calculating his chances of getting mounted men down there.

The slope consisted of yellow-gray soil and crumbling shale. At its immediate bottom was a drop-off of twenty feet into a narrow gulch. Farther upcountry, this drop-off had crumbled away, making a path over which a horse could travel. But the path was treacherous for riders. Against the danger Clee weighed the added mobility and effectiveness the troop would have once they did reach the bottom. *I'll see what Chivington says,* he thought, and settled back to wait.

About an hour passed. The Rebels in the cañon drowsed and lounged around. A half dozen of them played poker in the sunlight on a gray blanket. A man took off his pants down there and began to mend a hole in the seat. A fist fight broke out between two others, but an officer stopped it with a few curt words.

There was something — Clee stared, his jaw hardening. He had never seen Eames Jeffords in uniform. This officer wore a wide-brimmed, slouched hat. Yet there was something about the way he walked, the way he gestured with his hands. Clee wished fervently and futilely for binoculars. He glued his glance to the man.

The officer turned away from the sullen and glowering pair, and crossed to a wagon. He sat down in the shade, propping his back against the wheel. He took out a cigar and lighted up. Blue smoke was a light haze, drifting away from him.

Hate stirred in Clee, but it had not the intensity, the killing intensity he desired. So he let his mind drift into the past, let it dwell on Darrel, on the two treacherous duels Jeffords had fought there in Georgia so many years before. Clee thought of Sibyl, whom he might have had but for Jeffords's enslavement of her. His face flushed, and his anger rose, but it still was not enough. Not enough for killing, not enough to make him forsake his troop and his duty and seek Jeffords out personally. At last, he thought of Nanette, thought of the last words he had heard Jeffords say to him as he lay bound and beaten, a prisoner in Sam Massey's cabin: "Sometimes I think a little force. . . ." And he remembered Jeffords's sardonic laugh.

Nothing was sacred to Jeffords. And today he would die — would die by Clee's own hand. Clee's face was now white with his rage, rage that pounded slowly and powerfully through his body. A trooper came up behind him, saying in a low voice: "Major Chivington is going to attack, sir. He's been waiting for an hour, and he doesn't think they've laid a trap. He leaves it to your discretion, sir, whether you fight mounted or dismounted. He says to attack, when you see him move."

Clee turned his head, and nodded. He said: "All right. Send O'Rourke up here to me."

O'Rourke came on a run, hunched over.

Clee said: "Get them ready. We'll ride down the slope." He pointed to the sloughed-off bank of the ravine in the bottom. "We'll have to go down through there. That will bunch us pretty bad, so keep them strung out as they go down the slope."

O'Rourke was looking at him in puzzlement. He half opened his mouth to speak, then clamped it abruptly shut. Clee knew his tone and his words had left an impression with O'Rourke that Clee himself would not be along. This, indeed, had been what Clee had intended. He had thought to go down the slope first, ahead of the troop. He had intended to leave them at the gulch, to race into the Rebel camp and make certain of Jeffords. But it would not do. He knew it would not. His men would lose in confidence, if he left them. And a loss of confidence would cost many of them their lives.

Perhaps Jeffords would again escape. But even if he did, Clee could not betray these men who trusted him. They relied upon him to lead them, not to desert them in pursuit of private vengeance. A rolling rock on Chivington's slope caught his attention. He flung his glance over, saw the ragged blue line of troopers racing in gigantic strides down the steep and rocky slope. He sprang to his feet and, as O'Rourke led his horse to him, swung into the saddle.

He put the horse over the rim, and felt him plunge, haunch-sliding, down the slope. A hasty glance at the camp below showed their white, upturned faces, their utter surprise. He opened his mouth and let go a long, high yell. Behind him, the yell was echoed in a hundred throats. It was echoed again from the slope where Chivington's infantry slid pell-mell toward the bottom.

Clee could hear Eames Jeffords's shouting voice, rallying the Rebels in the bottom. From a knoll at the rear of the camp, a six-pounder, served by a dozen men, opened fire upon Chivington's column. Clee heard Chivington's bellow: "Captain Wyncoop! Take thirty men and silence that gun!"

Clee's animal reached the bottom first, and he slid the horse recklessly into the gulch, raising a cloud of fine, yellow dust. A horse behind him went down, pitching forward end over end, his rider springing nimbly clear. Clee halted in the shelter of the gulch to group his men, to give the last of them time to come off the slope. Then, waving his revolver, he rode up out of it at a run.

Jeffords's Confederates were forted up behind the wagons, except for a part of the teamsters who had vaulted onto the backs of the draft animals and mules and beat a swift retreat toward Santa Fé. Yelling, Clee's cavalry circled the corralled wagons. Chivington's force came up, taking positions surrounding the entire camp. Rifle fire crackled spasmodically from the gun emplacement on the knoll, and thereafter the gun was silent.

For the briefest while, both Chivington's and Clee's men poured a withering fire into the bunched wagons, fire which was answered half-heartedly by the defenders there. Then a voice bellowed — "Surrender!" — and white flags appeared in a dozen places, tied to the long barrels of rifles, white flags made of underwear, handkerchiefs, drawers, even white socks.

Chivington howled: "Throw down your arms, and come out with your hands up!"

At first the Rebels were timid and suspicious. A few came out, distrusting the Coloradoans, expecting to be shot down. When no shots were fired, they seemed to take heart. Others followed them, bearded, weary men, thin with too much marching and too little food.

Chivington bellowed: "Where the hell's that officer? Come out, damn you!"

Jeffords came out with his hands in the air. He was scowling bitterly. Clee rode close to him, looking down. He knew at once that he had been cheated again. He knew that perhaps he would never kill Jeffords now. And suddenly it did not seem to matter. Clee even managed to feel a little pity for Jeffords, for upon Jeffords's face was full consciousness of the enormity of what was happening here. Clee put it into words. "Even if you

229

win at Pigeon's, you have lost the West. An army can't fight without supplies. Where are the horses and the mules?"

Jeffords gave him a cold stare. "Find them."

Clee grinned. "We will." He turned away.

One of Chivington's troopers, rifle at ready, bayonet fixed, stepped toward Jeffords, saying: "Move along, you! Get over there with the rest of the prisoners."

Clee heard a shout, a warning shout. His heels instinctively dug at his horse's sides. His hand twitched at the reins, and his horse started to come around. Then, with frightening finality, something struck Clee on the shoulder blade, driving him forward across his horse's withers. He was dimly conscious that he was falling. Like an echo to the blow against his back came the crack of a small pistol. The world, sky and landscape, whirled fantastically before his glazing eyes. He heard the roar of a musket and smelled its acrid blast and, as he struck the ground, heard a trooper's vicious snarl — "You god-damned treacherous bastard!" — and the grunt of a man as a bayonet slid into his prone and struggling body. Clee's dazed mind fought for enough consciousness to realize what had happened. Dimly he could perceive that Jeffords had shot him in the back, probably with a small, hold-out gun. The trooper had in turn shot Jeffords with his rifle and then, out of pure outrage and disgust, had bayoneted him. With his last conscious awareness, he wondered if he would die, if

Jeffords would live. Then, all was black, and quiet, and peaceful.

Behind them, Chivington's men left a smoldering pile of charred wreckage where once had stood Sibley's hope of the conquest of the West. Eighty wagons, turned on their sides and set afire, sent a column of smoke a mile in the air. The horses, between five and six hundred, were located in a small gulch half a mile from the Rebel camp. And the slaughter began. Ammunition, which was growing scarce in Chivington's force, was deemed too valuable to use slaughtering horses. So until late afternoon the gulch was a horror of blood, struggling, sweating men, and shrieking horses as bayonets were utilized for the killing. Not a man but regretted the wanton slaughter. Yet they could not take the animals over the hazardous route they had just traversed, nor could they drive them through La Glorieta Pass for fear of having them retaken by the remnants of Sibley's Brigade.

At four, they toiled back up the slope which had been descended so swiftly but a few short hours before. As they climbed, a horseman dashed into the camp below from the direction of Pigeon's and whirled, dashing immediately back in the direction from which he had come.

Chivington turned to Wyncoop, grinning. "I don't know how the battle went at Pigeon's today, but that messenger is going to take the heart right out of the Rebs. Wouldn't surprise me any if they sent over a white flag before the night's out."

Clee, lashed to a travois behind his horse, regained and lost consciousness a dozen times on the long ride back to Koslowski's. Once a man walking beside him saw his open eyes, and said: "Lieutenant, that god-damn' Reb officer is dead, if that makes you feel any better."

Pain was a tangible presence, riding the travois with Clee. Blood soaked his clothes, soaked the hasty bandage which had been plugged into his wound. But the satisfaction that should have been present at the news of Jeffords's death was lacking. It was as though the whole reason for his living had been removed at one lightning stroke. He fought the pain and the dark shades of unconsciousness and, after what seemed a whole lifetime, felt his body lifted from the travois and carried into a building. Then, at last, there was utter lack of motion, and deep, drugged sleep.

Along the grassy banks of Cherry Creek, the cottonwoods were leafing out, their tiny, new leaves a pale, fresh green. Wedges of ducks and geese drove past overhead, heading north again, and they quacked noisily in the sloughs along the Platte as they settled to rest each night. Flinging mud high from its whirling wheels, Vic Levy's stage brought Sibyl McAllister back to Denver, subdued and timid, but repentant. She and Vic were married the following day.

Nanette, watching them drive away from the

church in Vic's black buggy, felt a deep sadness for Clee, but withal a certain hope aborning in her own heart. Clee could no longer have Sibyl. Perhaps. . . . Her full, soft lips firmed out, and her eyes grew still. A woman was a fool, when she continued to hope. With her shoulders sagging, she made her way back toward the Fremont House.

A courier had long since brought the news to Denver of Sibley's utter defeat at Apache Cañon, of the victory at Pigeon's which had been snatched away from him and nullified by the destruction of his wagon train. Nanette had anxiously scanned the lists of casualties, and her heart had died when she found both Sam and Clee among them. Only later had come the particulars, separating dead from wounded, and then Nanette had begun to live again, for both Sam and Clee had been among those wounded but not killed.

She looked up at the Stars and Stripes, flying so proudly from the tall flagpole atop the Fremont House. But for Clee and Sam, but for the gallant thousand who had marched out in early spring, that flag waving there would be the Stars and Bars of the Confederacy. Even now, they were coming back. Somewhere along the long, dim Santa Fé Trail, the ambulance wagons were moving north.

She went into the hotel lobby, and, as she crossed toward the stairs, the bespectacled clerk called: "Miss Massey!"

She turned, her glance questioning. The man said, smiling: "Have you heard the news?"

Nanette shook her head in amazement. The clerk's smile widened. "The ambulances are no more than ten miles from town. They'll be in this afternoon."

Blood drained from Nanette's face. Her breathing quickened. She whirled and, running, went out of the hotel.

The sun was warm upon her back. Excitement beat with a pulsing throb through her body. She raced down the street, skirts held high. At the corner she turned and, again, at the entrance to the Elephant Corral.

Ten minutes later, she drove out, lashing the back of the buggy horse with the long, light buggy whip. Recklessly she took the turn and bounced across the bridge. So much waiting, so long, and now it was over.

What would they look like? She expected them to be thinner. She expected beards. Beyond that she could not tell. But she knew how terrible, how agonizing must be the endless, jolting movement of the ambulance wagons.

She left Denver behind. Her buggy horse began to sweat, and she slowed him to a walk. Camp Weld passed behind her. Suddenly Nanette knew she should not have come. She knew the terrible truth that no woman should throw herself at any man. She thought angrily to herself: *I can say I came out to see Sam! He does not have to know that it was he I came to see!*

She was remembering the long weeks at the cabin on Cherry Creek, the night that had ended it. Her face flushed hotly at her memories. She was remembering Jeffords, who had been so insistent, who had cooled so quickly when she snatched his pistol from its underarm holster and dug its muzzle into his flat, hard belly.

Suddenly she saw them. Across the rolling grassland came the grim cavalcade, a dozen wagons, perhaps twenty horsemen. Their pace was slow, a steady crawl that spared the wounded all that it was possible to spare them. They rode wearily, exhaustion making them appear more like the defeated than the victorious. Their clothes were ragged and mud-spattered. Blanket strips, tied with leather thongs, encased their feet. The ribs of the horses stood out like basketwork, and a man could have hung his hat on the horses' hip bones.

Two rode out in front, two from whom Nanette could not tear her eyes. She drew her buggy to the side of the road. Were those two her Sam and Clee? Impossible. Yet it was true. In the eyes of both were dullness and complete disinterest in the shining buggy.

Tears glistened in Nanette's eyes. Her lower lip trembled. She almost sobbed her cry: "Clee! Sam!"

Surprise and disbelief were the things first seen in their eyes. Then they reined their horses toward her, and the ambulances rumbled past. Clee sat looking down at her, unmoving. His

235

eyes suddenly glistened with the light moisture of weakness, of relief. His shoulder and torso were bulky with dirty bandages. Grimacing, he dismounted, and, when he stood before her, his forehead was beaded with the sweat of pain and exertion. He raised a hand to her, and she alighted stiffly.

She said stolidly: "Clee, Sibyl married Vic Levy today. I just came from her wedding."

His eyes showed her no feeling at all. But they were hungry eyes, and humble ones.

She said, still stiffly: "Clee, I'm sorry."

He swayed a little, and grinned, his lips drawing tightly against his teeth. He put out his arms to her, and suddenly her face was close against the dirty shoulder of his uniform coat.

When he spoke, his voice was husky and hoarse from disuse: "Nan, there are ten thousand nights in a lifetime. With you and me, every one can be like the first."

Nan was crying without restraint. But her tears were compounded of the purest joy. Sam, staring down from his tall horse, smiled a moment and rode away.

About the Author

Lewis B. Patten wrote more than ninety Western novels in thirty years, and three of them won Golden Spur Awards from the Western Writers of America, and the author received the Golden Saddleman Award. Indeed, this points up the most remarkable aspect of his work: not that there is so much of it, but that so much of it is so fine. Patten was born in Denver, Colorado, and served in the U.S. Navy, 1933-1937. He was educated at the University of Denver during the war years and became an auditor for the Colorado Department of Revenue during the 1940s. It was in this period that he began contributing significantly to Western pulp magazines, fiction that was from the beginning fresh and unique and revealed Patten's lifelong concern with the sociological and psychological affects of group psychology on the frontier. He became a professional writer at the time of his first novel, MASSACRE AT WHITE RIVER (1952). The dominant theme in much of his fiction is the notion of justice, and its opposite, injustice. In his first novel it has to do with exploitation of the Ute Indians, but as he matured as a writer he explored this theme with significant and poignant detail in small towns throughout the early West. Crimes, such as rape or lynching, are often at the center of his stories. When the values embodied in these small towns are examined closely, they are found to be wanting. Conformity is always easier than taking a stand. Yet, in Patten's view of the American West, there is usually a man or a woman who refuses to conform. Among his finest titles, always a difficult choice, are surely A KILLING AT KIOWA (1972), RIDE A CROOKED TRAIL (1976), and his many fine contributions to Doubleday's Double D series, including VILLA'S RIFLES (1977), THE LAW AT COTTONWOOD (1978), and DEATH RIDES A BLACK HORSE (1978). No less noteworthy are his previous **Five Star** titles, TINCUP IN THE STORM COUNTRY and TRAIL TO VICKSBURG.

The employees of G.K. Hall hope you have enjoyed this Large Print book. All our Large Print titles are designed for easy reading, and all our books are made to last. Other G.K. Hall books are available at your library, through selected bookstores, or directly from us.

For information about titles, please call:

(800) 223-1244
(800) 223-6121

To share your comments, please write:

Publisher
G.K. Hall & Co.
P.O. Box 159
Thorndike, ME 04986